# Southword *42*

Southword is published
by Southword Editions
an imprint of the
Munster Literature Centre
Frank O'Connor House
84 Douglas Street
Cork City T12 X802
Ireland

www.munsterlit.ie

@MunLitCentre

/southwordjournal

/munsterliteraturecentre

#Southword

Issue 42
ISBN 978-1-905002-97-9

**Editor**
Patrick Cotter

**Seán Ó Faoláin International Short Story Competition Judge**
Simon Van Booy

**Gregory O'Donoghue International Poetry Competition Judge**
Thomas McCarthy

**Production**
James O'Leary

Thank you to Anne Kennedy for her technical assistance



Cover Image: *'Oileán' ('Island')* by Peadar Lamb

*The Munster Literature Centre is a grateful recipient of funding from*

the arts council
an chomhairle ealaíon
funding
literature
artscouncil.ie

Comhairle Cathrach Chorcaí
Cork City Council

# CONTENTS

# Please Subscribe

By subscribing, you will receive new issues of *Southword* straight from the printers, as quickly as we will ourselves. Your subscription will also help to provide us with the resources to make *Southword* even better.

***Rates for two issues per year:***

| | |
|---|---|
| Ireland, UK, USA | €20 *postage free* |
| Germany, France, Italy, Spain | €24 *postage free, tax-inclusive* |
| Rest of the world | €30 *postage included* |

For subscriptions and renewals visit munsterlit.ie.

*Southword* may also be purchased issue-by-issue through Amazon outlets worldwide and select independent booksellers.. We keep an up-to-date list of supporting bookshops on the munsterlit.ie subscriptions page.

# Reading Ilya Kaminsky
## Gerard Smyth

Between Akhmatova and Mandelstam
there is bookspace on the shelf for the poet from Odessa.
I must follow his verses back to where they sprang
like the first green shoots that rise out of the snow.
I must follow him back to his city of ancestors
where his bloodline ran
and all the old buildings were bleached in the sun.
These poems of his look me in the eye,
they are like a stiff breeze from the Black Sea.
I hold them to my ear and hear a polka.
It is music no bombardment can silence or kill,
no persecution can suppress with weaponry.
Just as in the days of early autumn
when it is time to rake the leaves, it's time again
to read the poet from Odessa, turn his pages
and hope to find a poem with a happy ending
in which I hear a beckoning shout from *Pushkin Street.*
Or one with wheat fields and a sunflower farm,
a grandmother making jam
with plums stolen from the highest branches.

## 1st Prize, Gregory O'Donoghue International Poetry Competition

### The Last Kodak Moment

Timothy McBride

*After losing 122,550 jobs, the Rochester, NY, company—founded by George Eastman and marked by its ubiquitous yellow logo—filed for bankruptcy on September 3, 2013.*

Like most invasive species, those first digital cameras
looked more or less benign: bulky, inept, confined,
to a small niche in the ecosystem, their quick
pixelated images no threat to our messy chemistry
of film and silver halide, the darkroom's nuanced shades.
Too late we noticed that our great Yellow Father was dying:
Kodacolor, Ektachrome, Kodachrome ("all the world's a sunny day"),
our slides and negatives, gelatin and emulsions—it was all immaterial now,
it was data and algorithms, numeric codes, calculators
affixed to a lens. It was dot patterns on a backlit screen,
no scent of the developing bath, no risk of exposure
to the invading light, no need to budget shots,
or pay for duplicates—the ammunition free
and infinite, instant results you could instantly retouch
(without touching) and circulate infinitely through the ether.
For a hundred years, we'd been a fixture at every wedding,
essential as the tree at Christmas, the cake at birthdays.
A stay against disappearance, our work began to disappear.
So we cleaned out our desks and lockers, trashed our badges,
carried our lives home in cardboard boxes. We staked FOR SALE signs
in our front lawns, learned the word "foreclosure."
We murdered each other in record numbers. We watched
the delis, gyms, and cafes we could no longer afford
flounder like pilot fish around a rotting host. We tried
not to think of George Eastman's "My work is done. Why wait?"
before he shot himself in the chest. But our work was done.

When they tore down the first of more than 90 buildings
along Lake Avenue, I waited, complicit, in a roped off
parking lot to watch the orderly implosion, craning my neck
as I aimed to preserve a final keepsake of our lives,
blasted to bits and stored on my telephone.

## Operating Room

James Finnegan

I think it was Francis McNutt's *Healing*
    before or after he left the priesthood
which nudged my mind from an either/or cell
through an open door to a both/and world
    or at least its possibility
as sometimes the choice is between two things
    as in *wanted dead or alive*
but let's assume none are being hunted

I have seen Charles Simic offer a choice
    at the end of a work
say between someone talking or singing
    or in another work    the choice between
lingering over drinks or heading home
    and long before that
John Fowles in *The French Lieutenant's Woman*
provides two different endings    that was

nineteen sixty-nine when many wondered
would The Beatles break up or not
    and long memory
keeps putting them back together again
two gone    not half the group they used to be
and the shadow cast comes from more than one thing
        thank you Mary Oliver
    in the other direction    there's *only* one thing

which can back one into a corner
    a modern-day Isaiah has given

his anti-monist take on
'The Pursuit of the Ideal'
while Paul Simon proposes fifty ways
to leave a lover
and finally the song and dance man sings
'It's either one or the other or neither of the two.'

# 3rd Prize, Gregory O'Donoghue International Poetry Competition

## Ruritanian Episode
*A Fable of Sorts*
Seán Hickey

Then there was the war.
Border skirmishes;
an all out three years
with the Moldravians.

Their hussars had bigger moustaches
and shinier buttons on their tunics,
their ponies were sleeker,
more deftly shod,
their cannon less likely
to explode in one's face.

We lost.
We had to cede
our westernmost provinces
and the port city of 'L'
but we survived.

Our poets are still writing
their epics of defeat
in coffee houses and garrets,
our schoolchildren sing
tearful patriotic songs
walking arm in arm
in the municipal parks,
our beloved flag
wavers at half mast
over palaces and ministries.

In the cathedral, the archbishop's sermons
are almost decorous in their restraint.

The statues of our generals
retain a martial demeanour
under verdigris and pigeon shit.
Duelling is back in fashion.

We're considering sending
an ambassador again
to the Moldravian capital.
We're mulling it over.

## A MISSING PIECE OF TERRITORY / BREAKS BOUNDARIES AND AGGREGATE WATERS

Mara Adamitz Scrupe

in a spare narrow four-room energetically peak-roofed
farmhouse – on eighty acres at Verndale Minnesota – lacking pipes
or ductwork or wiring – Grandma Cecilia bade me stand naked in a tin
tub set on the linoleum floor next to the wood-stoked cookstove & I waited
willingly for the bliss of hot to wash over me for my skin to color crimson

///

Midway between Howardsville & Columbia we put in at Shores
on the James/ it's May/ there's been rain the likes of which comes
this time of year in an avalanche of opacity/ the river's up & as for borders
we're between them/ Fluvanna County to the north/ Latin-named
for an English queen & Buckingham to the south after a village
in that country paddling pulling hard approaching fast the boulders
of Class II rapids rough hit straight on/ thrown into the churn
we nearly lose our brand-new canoe & with that blow to the bow we gain
a crenellated furrow/ a notch cut in victory by this rowdy river

///

I am a North Shore girl & in the instance of the dissolution
of my first marriage I make for the Lake lake lake & lake
there is so much of it where the Edmund Fitzgerald rests or did
but it's summer spreading a blanket across an articulated puzzle

of bouldered beach/ cragged uncomfortably at my back/ quartz
crammed crystalline & glittering in black basalt fissures a fine
afternoon with you on top notwithstanding the continent's best effort
– a billion years past – to split in half right here

///

the largest freighter ever to sail the Great Lakes broke apart on Lake Superior
in the massive waves of a November gale at around 7:30 in the morning of
November 9th 1975 the huge ship went down in 530 feet of water off
Whitefish Point Minnesota in the captain's last communication

he reported *We are holding our own.* to which an officer in a vessel
ten miles distant replied *Okay, fine. I'll be talking to you later.*

///

as noted I am a North Shore girl in all the disparate populousnesses
of snows – in form crystallized December – camped at Bearskin Lake
thirty-seven miles north of Grand Marais close by the Canadian border
& the heat is skiing *skiing* over solid lake to the beer joint
at the far shore & the heat hot *hot*
of a new man's love & what I recall bodily – pulling off jacket
& woolen sweater & scarf & settling/ skirring along/ in silk long
underwear – as that fever/swelter raw of wintriness

## Etude no. I

Kim Curts Mattheussens

they gently removed their calloused clothes
in a double room in Paris. she met him

on the bathroom floor. the clawed feet
of the milk blue porcelain tub rested

in the $19^{th}$ century. tiles were tiny bleached
squares of bone. in the bath, there lay

a piano, half underwater. she played
its keys in muted treble caresses.

he placed his thumbs on middle c.
one hand mirrored the other, *andante,*

steadily, moving opposite with light touch,
then rushing back to collide again.

the gold and black striped wallpaper trembled
as a *sonatina* drifted out the window.

## Breaking Up

Frank Farrelly

*The Museum of Broken Relationships is a museum in Zagreb, Croatia, dedicated to failed love relationships. Its exhibits include personal objects left over from former lovers, accompanied by brief descriptions.*

In the foyer a busker belts out *Love Me Do.*
The cashier smirks like she knows a sucker
when she sees one. You stop to study every object

—I glance perfunctorily, indulge a little schadenfreude,
continue to the next. Soon we lose each other
in the labyrinth. I circle back to the museum shop,

all its corny merchandise, buy a coffee,
find myself imagining you met someone
between the furry handcuffs and the rubber pig,

someone who fills some lack you mourn in me:
inattention to detail, conclusion-jumping to a fault.
My head spins, panic-wrenched I am already

agonising what to mark our break;
that Beatles hit, this overpriced latte,
when you appear, radiant in the dark mouth

of the maze. I perk up like a child, gather myself,
wave palely as an effete poet
too wearied by the world to even fake a smile.

## Hang-glider in the Comeraghs
Peggy McCarthy

I watch him catch currents of air,
a wide-winged bird wafts above summits.
Below, the gurgle of deep-throated gullies,

the clasp of heather on clay
where rushes fatten in dank soil,
centuries of life bed soft as a resting lung.

Overhead he dazzles in sunlight,
silent, solitary,
carefree as Icarus before the fall.

Yet I suspect a Daedalus somewhere,
one who whooshed him to the heavens.
A face tilts like mine, squints,

watches him lift, risk himself to the sky
away and afloat to the north,
rowing with wings, out of sight.

Up ahead he'll drop to earth again,
scramble to catch the rush of ground
sliding backwards beneath his feet.

(Ref: Aeneid Book 6, Seamus Heaney)

## Born Opposite

Jim McElroy

*for Jean Bleakney*

Fed handed-down fears from the prams of our lives.
Behind these daubed walls, false gods, higher spires,
the smoulder of tyres, fuming pyres, Molotovs.
On the breeze-carried beat, the throb of the drum,
hurled abuse of our youth, tongues barbed as our wire.
Beyond the cross roads, marked yards of our kerbs,
rubbled flags, foreign banners rise hills like an anthem
to a fever of eyes round monument, wreath.
Past parish march-ditch, furrowed soil of our farms,
through the ups and the downs of our drumlins,
where forefathers fought for these perches of earth,
for our landed birthright, first claim for the clan –
watch our rioted nights flare uprisings and settings,
feuding warlords stain bleeding red lines on horizons.

Feuding warlords stain bleeding red lines on horizons:
watch our rioted nights flare uprisings and settings,
for our landed birthright, first claim for the clan.
Where forefathers fought for these perches of earth,
through the ups and the downs of our drumlins,
past parish march-ditch, furrowed soil of our farms,
to a fever of eyes round monument, wreath –
rubbled flags, foreign banners rise hills like an anthem.
Beyond the cross roads, marked yards of our kerbs –
hurled abuse of our youth, tongues barbed as our wire.
On the breeze-carried beat, the throb of the drum,
the smoulder of tyres, fuming pyres, Molotovs.
Behind these daubed walls, false gods, higher spires,
fed handed-down fears from the prams of our lives.

## Women's Work

Jamie O'Halloran

Where the Burmese sky should be, a stave
Of laundry lines wears a composition of female notes:
Panties and *htamein*—the woman's sarong—
Knotted on ropes crisscrossing above the protest
Zone instead of cradling hips. Feminine garments
Swell, full as if inhabited. Female flags
Of paisley, indigo, silk, wave in dissent, bearing
The substance of woman powerful enough to draw
A man's essence out of him the way north pulls
The needle home. To be female is to be a weapon.
Cloth defends the women of Myanmar
Who have no weapon against the military more potent

Than its own fear of being bootless, without luck,
Unmanned. Until the soldier lit the match.

## Nairobi, 1975

Ava Patel

The air is humid. But not
in a way that bothers you.

Laughter coats your ears
and there's the faintest trace
of bourbon on your breath.

The black satin of your dress
waves and winks like water.

And earlier, there were candles on a cake.

We feel excited.
Like a single butterfly
is twisting around our sternums.

The polaroid that's trapped you
still smells of joy.

I am drawn to a bare shoulder;
the smoothness of it,
the light that it absorbs and reflects.
The skin so silky it must be honey.
It tells me that there are things
to be revealed or remembered. Not sure which.

## Blind Field

Andrea Ward

There was no stopping her, returning to her marriage
bungalow built in the lower half of *Garraí Caoch*,
the 'Blind Field' sloping between bog and narrow road,
in sight of her childhood home turned outhouse.
She shouldn't but must work, standing on swollen
feet at the kitchen sink, facing the ewes and newborn
lambs and, uphill under the ash trees, the circular
ridge of ground, stone-studded, ancient eye sealed.

*Stone mined by levellers of forest, shaped as axes,*
*sharded as arrow-heads, stone hauled for hearth*
*and boundary and shrine, sunk in bog-rise,*
*delved again for anvil and quern and sacred circle.*

Working within her, faster than her will is fierce,
rebel flesh of her flesh is infiltrating, unravelling her.
People visit, bringing food and gossip. In the farmyard
her husband and son attend the business of birthing.
Fabric of generations, her memory of prayers, histories,
wildflowers is fraying. Like the fuchsia-red bedspread
spun in the old house from wool of their own sheep.
Her father conceived under it. She too, probably.

*She, flesh of their flesh – her infant uncles and aunts*
*tucked in a little swaddling under soil, limbo-bound*
*in the corner of a field, blind field. Bones like*
*stones, but flimsier: infant bones chalking, settling.*

Just fields away, her mother's house, its stones
packed like entrails, purple, pink, spud-coloured,
scruffed with limewash and lichen; the gap between
lintel and sill framing brambles and the willow tree
rising from the bedroom by the puddled road. Detail
in an old photo: her mother, a barefoot child, holding
in her name her own mother and dead sister, *Bridget,*
*Bridgie.* Within and without, which is which in ruin?

*Given a body, feel it reach, hold fast to urge and word*
*and story, feel it falter, chink by chink in wind and light,*
*dwelling milled by slippage, ground to earth for root*
*and stalk, food and flower for sheep and bee and child.*

## On the Latin Bridge

Sarah Wright

1985, changing trains in Sarajevo
no time for a coffee, just had to get out
and run across platforms, ticket in hand
heading for Venice, head full of Europe
too rushed and too young
to think of Franz Ferdinand.

To think of when Princip shot Franz Ferdinand
on the Latin Bridge in Sarajevo –
Gavrilo Princip, named after an angel, too young
to be hanged, was locked up and never got out
but he started a war that spilled out of Europe.
Did he think it had got out of hand?

1969, with a sixpence in my hand.
Grandad coughs in a bucket, and talks of Franz Ferdinand
and 1914 and the war in Europe
when he fought among poplars, far from Sarajevo
joined up at fourteen, got gassed and got out
lungs wrecked and still young.

2003, and young
Tsoritsa is clutching my daughter's hand
at the Wiener Prater on a school day out
among the green alleys where Franz Ferdinand
drove his carriage. Does Tsoritsa miss Sarajevo?
1939 saw another war in Europe,

1991 saw another war in Europe.
Tsoritsa must be too young
to recall the siege of Sarajevo,
Tsoritsa clutching my daughter's hand.
She knows nothing of Franz Ferdinand
but she knows that she had to get out.

People just had to get out
so they fled to the heart of Europe
the home of the Habsburgs where Franz Ferdinand
caroused when he was young
before his encounter with the Black Hand.
And I've never quite been to Sarajevo.

She's singing along to Franz Ferdinand, *Take Me Out.*
Maybe she'll see Sarajevo, maybe she'll tour Europe,
she's young, ticket in hand.

## Charging

Enda Wyley

*for Dermot Bolger*
*& in memory of Michael Hartnett*

Before the light goes out
on this phone, before
the scramble for a plug,
and the white box flashes
and the battery charges

before the blind is rolled up
and the light angles
its way into my room –
before all this,
for these fading minutes
let me listen and watch.

You are sitting
in your tweed suit
dressed up complete
with waistcoat
to honour your friend,
his poems in hand.

It is morning and he is standing
in a phone box on Leeson Street
pressing button A, calling you.
A joke. A new poem. Beady-eyed,
until the line dies, his money spent.

Oh, Angela Liston,
oh, father that he kissed
for the last and first time,
oh, woman that he loved
from the moment she died.

I hear it all now. The past opens
its pages, unearths him, stick cut
from a tree in Coole Park guiding
him home to Dartmouth Square.
My phone dies. The day charges.

# Photographs by John Minihan of writers at the Cork International Short Story Festival over the years

Self-portait,
2017

Simon Van Booy
(winner of the 2009
Frank O'Connor
Short Story Award)

Danielle McLoughlin, 2017

Conal Creedon, 2017

David Means, 2017

Nuala O'Connor, 2017

Lucy Caldwell, 2016

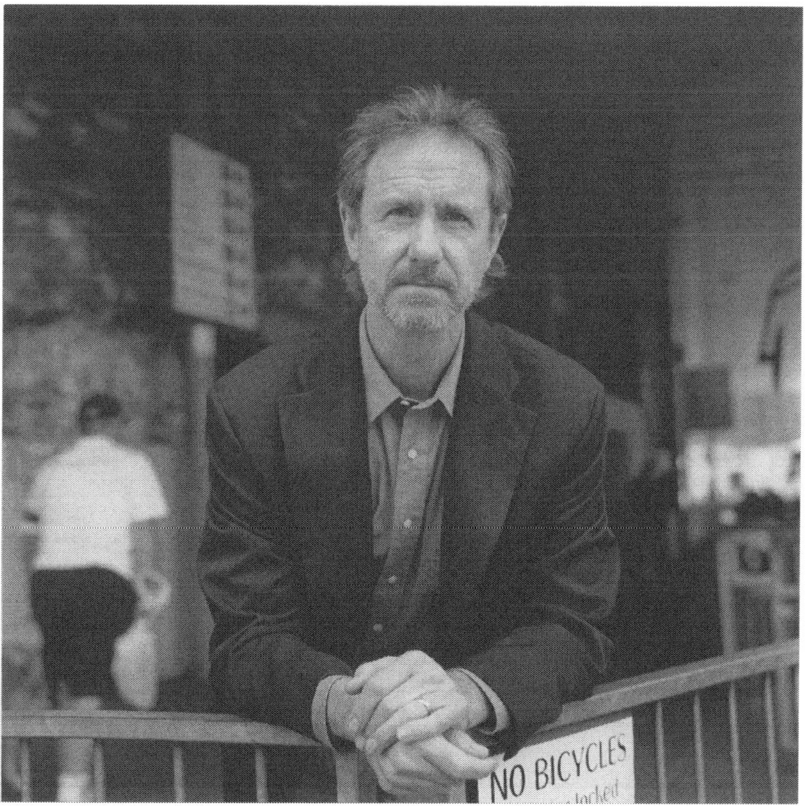


Ron Rash (winner of the 2010 Frank O'Connor Short Story Award)

Mary Costello with Ann Pancake, 2016

Salley Vickers, 2014

Zsuzsi Gartner (2016 Frank O'Connor International Short Story Fellow)

Ben Greenman with Karen Russell, 2010

Colin Barrett (winner of the 2014 Frank O'Connor Short Story Award)

Edna O'Brien (winner of the 2011 Frank O'Connor Short Story Award)

Steven Heighton, 2013 (recently deceased)

Alan McMonagle, 2013

Alistair MacLeod, 2013

ZZ Packer, 2009

Kristiina Ehin, 2014

## AGAINST DIAGNOSIS (2)

griffin epstein

in what facilitated conversation
will my cracked shell become an instrument
brain a diagnosable disorder

in which new diet will i find my soul?

just kidding, i don't think like that anymore

i'm supposed to make threats now:

if you swallow me, you'll be in trouble
i spill like blame by accident, all my boundaries
screaming hot

they call this "better"
i no longer need metaphor
know no one is special or beautiful
but for the economy of cliché

still, it's hard to be present
or take life as a present
forever mistaking a shadow in the corner
for some hurt that i can fix

the workbook calls this "the challenge of psychological pain
for creatures with language"

we ache to bring the petty world under
contextual control

i am not above it
even now i am
flooding the air with grammar
speaking these words as if they show that
i am cured

## Women's Studies circa 1986

Wes Lee

The saints with bright blue eyes
and starving mouths. The medieval mystics

who lived for Christ.

I was transfixed
by the girl who ate one wafer and lived for years

on pure devotion.

She wore a ring

and wasn't it a way of getting out of a real marriage
the lecturer said.

I remember the Sworn Virgins of Albania, who took on
the lives of men (when there was no male heir) —

dressed in their clothes, while the women
scrubbed floors,

they stare out of old photos, chewing cigars
and playing cards,

whiskey on their breaths.

# Am I Helping?
## Shelley Hastings

1[st] Prize, Seán Ó Faoláin International Short Story Competition

She was dying. I was visiting all the time. Every single week for months on end I took the bus to Bristol from London Victoria. It was cheap and slow. The station smelt of cigarettes and fried food. I liked the fuggy energy. I wanted to be delayed.

In December it was her sixty-second birthday. I left early and got drenched getting her a present in town. I stuffed the bag under my dripping raincoat. I was putting on weight. I looked like I was expecting. At bay nine a group of us waited for the coach driver to get off his phone. When he saw my stomach, he let me on first. I sat near the front and balanced my muffin on my lap. The heat pumped out of the grates and made my shins itch.

An old man with saggy eyes sat down next to me. He smelt of sweat and pastry. He wedged his holdall under one knee and had his other leg at an angle blocking the aisle. The engine started and I stared out of the window. When we got to the motorway I started to cry. This always happened.

The old man nudged my knee. His trousers were too short. I looked at the rectangle of flesh above his ankle. 'What's the matter?' he said.

I shook my head and wiped my face with my napkin. 'Life!'

He looked past me out the window at the fields flashing past.

'True enough,' he said.

Later, he pulled a paper bag out of his holdall and untwisted the top. It was a bag of sweet peanuts. He sucked on one loudly and offered them up.

'Help yourself, Pet,' he said.

I took two that were stuck together.

'That's better.' He smiled. 'Those chunky ones are the best.'

At the nursing home Sherry was on the bench outside smoking. She wasn't wearing a coat, just her lilac uniform and a reindeer scarf. Her hair was thin, and her teeth were too big for her mouth.

'Your Mum's at the hospital.' She pulled her scarf tightly around her.

I took the Debenhams bag out from under my coat.

'What's in there?' she said.

'Mum's birthday present.'

She stubbed the cigarette on the wall and put the butt in her pocket. She pressed her fob against the buzzer.

Inside she blew into her hands. 'It's arctic out there but like a sauna in here,' she said.

I followed her to reception. There was a tin of Quality Street open on the desk. 'Fill your boots,' she said. 'I won't eat them.'

I picked out a handful and stuffed them in my bag. Sherry was like a stick, her elbows at sharp angles. I stood behind her as she unlocked the door.

'No-one's been in since lunch,' she said.

There was a faint smell of urine. The bed was unmade. I could see a soiled pad curled up in the sheets. Out the window a garden chair I bought for the courtyard was lying on its side. I felt exhausted. I wanted to lie on the floor. I flopped onto the chair next to the bed. Sherry opened the window and cold air blew in.

'They couldn't get hold of you.'

'I was on the coach.' I touched the back of my hair. It was still damp from the rain.

'It was a locum. He wouldn't listen to me. He said it was an emergency. She needed the drip.'

'Don't worry.' I unzipped my raincoat and bits of muffin fell onto the floor.

Sherry was biting the corner of her nails. 'They'll bring her back later. We can do a cake in the residents' lounge.'

'She's diabetic.'

'I'll put up some balloons,' Sherry said. She touched the bone under her eye.

On the side was a Christmas card with a cartoon Santa. I picked it up and read the message.

'Thanks, Sherry,' I said. 'Are you doing anything for Christmas?'

'I'm working.'

A moaning sound was coming from the corridor.

'I'm sorry,' I said.

'I need the money. I've got New Year off, but I'll have to stay indoors. Buddy doesn't like the fireworks.' Her beeper went off but she didn't look at it.

'Buddy?'

'He's my rescue pup.' She pulled out a keyring and showed me a picture of a small scruffy dog with its tongue sticking out.

'Cute,' I said.

'He's like my bloody baby.'

On the floor was a blue plastic tray with a sippy cup and a plate of lunch, a mound of green mash and a plastic tub of jellied fruit covered in custard. I touched the top of the pudding with my finger.

'It's disgusting,' Sherry said. 'No one should have to eat that.' She picked up the tray and left it outside the door. An alarm sounded in the corridor.

'I better go. I'll come back later and change the bed.'

After she left, I took two Codeine and lay on the carpet. I could see Mum's slipper wedged under the mini fridge.

I took a taxi to the hospital. The road was dark and wet. I opened the window a crack and pressed my cheek against the cold glass. I listened to the tyres peeling over the tarmac. We passed the high stone wall of Ashton Court. I looked at the suspension bridge, the lines of it glittering across the gorge. There were Christmas lights like spiders' webs down Park Street. The shops were closing. The town centre was full of people going home, sticks of paper poking out of their bags.

She was in the yellow zone on floor D. I stopped at the Costa and bought a marshmallow snowman with chocolate buttons. I ate it standing in the foyer before I got into the lift.

The ward nurse was doing the drugs round, putting multicoloured pills into paper cups.

'Yum,' I said, and asked where Mum was.

She locked up her trolley.

'Bed five.' She glanced at her watch. 'Visiting hours are over in twenty minutes.'

My trainers squeaked on the laminate floor. I pulled at the blue plastic curtain, trying to find the gap.

Mum was lying flat, her hair a mess on the pillow. Her good hand was balled up hitting her chest. Someone had put a scratchy towel as padding in the way. I held her fist and uncurled her fingers. Her nails were long.

'Happy Birthday,' I said, and kissed the top of her hand. 'We should cut these.'

She bared her teeth. She looked wild. She held my arm tightly, her nails digging in. 'Help,' she mouthed. 'Help me, help me.' She whispered it over and over like a spell. Her eyes were yellow. She had thick bubbles of spit in the corners of her mouth.

'I'm here now. I'm going to ask them to discharge you.'

Her lips were still moving but no sound was coming out. I pulled the sheet up around her, smoothed it down and tucked her in. I put my hand on her chest and held it there. She let out a long sigh like a balloon deflating, then closed her eyes.

The doctor was Italian. She had curly dark hair and was wearing a polo neck, her lanyard swinging. She took me to her office. The room was small and windowless. Papers and files were piled up on her desk. She turned her chair to face me and crossed her legs as she spoke. She had a turquoise pendant and a solid shelf of breast. I felt myself leaning towards her. I noticed her hair was dyed red in her photo ID.

'Please. Have I explained that all clearly enough?' she said.

I swallowed hard. My head was hurting.

She turned, rubbed the back of her neck, and picked up a folder from her desk. 'It's her birthday today,' I said. 'Can we get her back?'

They wheeled her bed through the corridors. The walls were pale green and scuffed with wavy lines. Nurses wearing Santa hats hurried past. She had four orange belts strapped across her body to keep her in place. They had given her morphine. I wondered if she could see anything or if everyone seemed like ghosts. The ambulance was empty. They pushed her bed up the ramp and I sat on the fold-down seat and rested my hand on her foot.

When I was small, Mum played this game where she made this zooming noise when she drove me around, as if the police were chasing her. She would tense up her shoulders and clutch the wheel. She was actually driving very slowly, but at each corner she screeched, and eventually the sirens came, the 'nee naw nee naw,' and she would park at the supermarket and put her arms in the air to surrender. Only then would she turn and look at me. 'The games up!' she'd say, 'they've finally got me.' I hated and loved it all at once.

The driver arrived pushing an elderly man in a wheelchair. He parked him opposite me and clipped him in. The man's face was creased like paper. He had a sour, pickled smell. His chin was on his chest and he was wearing a stained leather jacket with nothing underneath.

'Merry Christmas,' I said. He remained slumped and silent.

The driver started the engine and looked back at me and winked. He was a huge man, bald and red faced. The seams strained on his high-vis jacket.

'All right back there?' he said.

'These two are conked out,' I said.

The driver's name was Mikey. He said he worked for a private company, not the NHS. 'I'm plugged in if anything happens.' He gestured to the radio. 'I'm a transportation service. I'm dropping Mr O'Connor first, all good?'

We drove through Hartcliffe and the estates of Knowle West. Mikey talked the whole time. He said he had just bought a wreck in Backwell with a nice piece of land, an investment. 'I don't know what I'm going to do with it yet. There's an outhouse. It came with chickens. I could rent it out as storage. I'm still thinking about it.' He said his mum lived in Spain and that his sister had moved to Glasgow. 'You married?' he said.

'No.'

'Fair enough. I've never managed to settle down.'

'Will you go to Spain for Christmas?'

'Can't leave my dogs,' he said. 'What you doing?'

'Not sure yet.'

'Oh, bless you.' He glanced back at Mum. Her face was lit up by the pale orange streetlights. He pulled into a car park next to a housing estate.

'Right. Mr O'Connor?' he said. He clapped his hands.

Mr O'Connor didn't wake up. Mikey jumped out, opened the doors and let down the ramp. 'Come on old boy. I don't want any trouble.' He laughed a wheezy laugh as he pulled the wheelchair backwards down the ramp. Mr O'Connor's head lolled to the side.

'Is he okay?'

Mikey mimed downing a pint.

'Are you dropping him with someone?' I said.

'It's a halfway house. I'll be two minutes.' He pulled up the ramp and shut the doors.

There was a lighter on the floor where Mr O'Connor had been sitting. I picked it up, shook it, then tried the flint. It sparked four times then lit. I stared at the flame floating in the darkness until my eyes watered. My thumb was burning. I looked at Mum. She was completely still, her tiny body barely there. Shadows flickered across the floor.

'Is this it?' I said.

I listened to the clicks the engine was making, holding the warm lighter in my fist. After a while I unclipped my seatbelt and put my hand on her chest. She was still breathing. I tucked the blanket around her legs.

'Not long now,' I said. I sat back down.

Eventually the door clunked open and Mikey slid a folded-up wheelchair down one side. I held out the lighter in my palm.

'Mr O'Connor dropped this,' I said.

'He's good for it. I'll keep it. I'll be seeing him again.'

'Did he wake up?'

'Oh yeah.' He smiled. 'He woke up when I took away his chair!'

We drove back through town. Mikey talked about his work, how he had been a supervisor on construction sites in his twenties then moved into security.

'I did nights at Cabot Circus when they were building it. I hated it. I prefer this, at least you get to talk to people. I want to feel like I'm helping. Am I helping?' He laughed. 'You still awake back there?'

'I am,' I said. 'Sorry. You are helping. I know what you mean.'

He parked in front of the nursing home in the emergency bay. I waited for him to let us out, but he reached over to the dashboard and started flicking through his phone. 'I want to show you something. You won't believe it,' he said.

'What?'

'Hang on. Honestly. You are not going to believe this.'

He handed me his phone and I looked at the screen. It was a photograph of a photograph. A professional black and white shot of a muscular man with an oiled chest and white teeth. His jeans were open, so you could see the cuts of his muscles on his abs.

'Who's that?' I said.

He grinned.

'Is it you?' I looked again. 'You look like Arnold Schwarzenegger.' I handed the phone back.

'I used to do competitive body building when I was a teenager. Mountain Mike.'

'Wow.'

He studied it, zooming in on his muscles. 'I'm nineteen in this picture.'

I looked at his smiling face lit up from his phone. He didn't move.

I squeezed Mum's ankle. 'Mountain Mike,' I said. 'Can we go inside?'

Mikey let down the ramp. He banged each shoulder, his breath making clouds. 'It's a bit nippy, ladies,' he said.

The lights from the foyer made the pavement sparkle. There was a knitted nativity display in the window. Sherry was standing next to the three kings, wearing the scarf she had on earlier, holding a balloon.

Inside there was a birthday banner pinned on her door. Mikey undid the orange straps with Sherry and lifted her onto the bed.

'You're as light as a feather, Madam,' he said.

Mum was somewhere far away. She looked peaceful on the clean white sheets. The floor had been vacuumed. There was a caterpillar cake in a box and bunting strung across the wall.

'Thanks for all this, Sherry,' I said.

'It's no bother.' She fiddled with her scarf.

Mikey just stood there. His body took up half the room.

'Do you need to get back, Mikey?' I said.

He shuffled in his boots. 'No rush. You got everything you need?'

'Should we eat the cake?' I said.

'Not for me,' Sherry said.

I cut a thick slice for Mikey and we ate it standing around Mum's bed.

When he had finished Mikey wiped his hands on his jacket. 'Right.' He patted his chest. 'You take care.' He took my hand in his meaty fist and shook it. He gave Mum a salute.

'Merry Christmas,' I said.

Sherry was looking out the window. 'It's supposed to snow tonight,' she said.

'Is it now?' Mikey said. 'Well, there you go.' He peered over her shoulder into the dark.

After they left, I ate more cake. I drank the apple juice out the carton from the fridge. Mum was making a whistling noise as she slept.

'Mum. I've bought you something,' I said.

I knelt next to the bed. I bit off the tags and laid it out. It was a dressing gown, its synthetic fleece as soft as rabbit fur. I put the hood next to her face and touched her cheek.

'Wake up.'

I shook her gently. She opened her eyes wide for a second and took me in.

'Help me,' she murmured. 'Help me.' Her fist started up again.

'I'm trying,' I said.

Later, snow fell. I put on her new dressing gown and went outside.

# Requiem for a Strip Club

## Neil Cawley

2nd Prize, Seán Ó Faoláin International Short Story Competition

It's not how I planned my life. Sitting in a dark room watching women take their clothes off for money. Me. Jimmy Murphy. St. Anne's High School Class of '89. Strip Club King of Queens. I never got used to it, even after nearly thirty years in the business. Mom dreamed of me becoming the first American pope. That didn't exactly work out. When I was a kid I figured I'd be a cop. Then the '80s hit. Money was everywhere. We all had the same dream back then – get a job on Wall Street, live in the city and make a fortune. And for all you newbies who don't know any better, "the city" is Manhattan. Not Brooklyn, not Queens, not anywhere else. Manhattan. I'm so tired of these hipsters in Astoria telling me how they love living in the city. You're in the outer boroughs, got it? I was an outer borough guy myself, born and raised in Howard Beach. Nothing wrong with that. We were the only Irish family surrounded by Italians in Mobland. We had ours, they had theirs, but theirs was way cooler and most times we ended up working for them anyway.

I got here the easy way. My dad dies two days after his fifty-first birthday. Heart attack. I'm twenty and the whole thing falls on me. So I drop out of college and look for a job to take care of mom and my sister Deirdre.

But that's where things get interesting. This old timer on the block, Sammy, waves me over one day. Dad used to yell at me to stay away from people like Sammy. I never said a word to him my whole life and here he is waving at me. So I go over. He puts his arm around me and pulls me in close. And he's got that old man smell. His eyes are watery, his voice shaky. I can tell. He's been here.

Sammy tells me, "You got it bad. I know. I know everything goes on here. It's what I do in retirement. Some men golf. I watch. I see everything. It's all a mess. Your dad was a good man. Bit of a drinker like you people can be. A little gambling, but no women. I saw. I know."

I know about Sammy too. It was rumored he was a hitman for the local family that ran things in the neighborhood, and that he killed the guy who accidentally ran over a mobster's son on Cross Bay Boulevard years ago. That guy was never seen again. Disappeared. People started whispering, "it was Sammy done that." All over the neighborhood. So he's got my attention.

Sammy says he knows some "businessmen" on Queens Boulevard. "They're opening a club," he tells me. "You know, one of them strip clubs. But real nice. Velvet ropes. You gotta pay to get in. And they need someone with muscle. I've seen you handle yourself. Not very big but you're fast." It was the first time in my life anyone talked to me like that. Like I was a man. Sammy knew something that would take me years to figure out. I became a man the day my father died. "Sure, I'm in," I tell Sammy. "Thanks for thinking of me."

That was the only time we ever spoke.

I get the call and start working at *Liaisons*. Classy, right? It's like I've died and gone to heaven. The girls are gorgeous. I don't want to take a day off. I work security so I shake down the drunks and the losers who show up with no money. At first I get physical real fast but then my boss Sal shows me how to size them up before they hit the door and send them off with a look.

It doesn't take long for Sal to see I got a brain. I stop staring at the girls and focus on the business instead. I ask questions about what's going on and come up with ideas he likes. Pretty soon he brings me inside and I start managing. Even the guys Sal answers to notice. It takes a while but they start talking to me too.

Sal tells me it's all about the girls, not because we're gentleman but because they're the talent. That's what Sal calls them, "the talent". Maybe it makes it easier. He's got daughters of his own so that's how he gets through the day. "Nobody puts their hands on the talent!" he yells. "I don't want any of the talent bringing any drugs into my establishment!" But "the talent" are real girls with real names and I have a hard time calling them by their stage names like he wants me to. My Catholic guilt pops up from time to time. It's not a good way to make a living. But I stay for the money like everyone else.

I miss Sal. I really do. We had some good times together. Maybe you heard what happened but I'll tell you anyway. I'm closing out the money one night. Sal asks me take it with me and put it in the bank the next day. He doesn't like to keep cash at the club. So I'm driving home with a few grand in my bag. I'm living by the beach in Rockaway back then. I'm listening to freestyle to stay awake. I'm thinking about asking out one of the girls, Marisol. She's amazing and we get along great, but I'm worried what Sal might say.

I park in front of my building, and I get jumped as soon as I get out of the car. It happens so fast. One guy nails me from behind, the other belts me across the head. But I stay on my feet. I start coming back at the smaller one with some nice jabs, and I hear a gun go off. I know I'm hit. I just know. My brain races to find where I've been shot before I feel it so I can brace myself. Like when you stub your toe and look at it just before the pain kicks in. My mind and body get to the same place at exactly the same time. My left leg! The pain is incredible. I go down. I'm just staring at my leg while they take off with the cash. It's July and I'm shaking with the chills. I can't even speak. The only thing I remember is the sun rising on the water. Gorgeous sunrise. And if it's the last good thing I ever see, I guess I can't complain.

I wake up in the hospital. Mom's crying. She didn't take too well to my career choice. Deirdre's there too. We say nothing. Mom puts a rosary beads in my hand and tells me the Virgin Mary will keep me safe. God love her. Not much else is said because even if I know something I'm not talking. Days go by. The cops come in and I keep it brief. I'm being legit, I don't remember.

So I get out of the hospital and learn to get around. No word from the club. Nothing from Sal. Weird, right? I'm not calling him. He can come see me after all I done for him. I finally go back to work a few weeks later when I'm stronger. And I'm ready to lay into Sal. But no Sal. Days go by. No Sal. Just a bunch of goombahs coming in running things and no one says anything because we all know who's in charge. Different day, different face. They put me on a stool at the door to check IDs. Don't let me anywhere near the cash. And they're watching me. I can feel it.

Then comes the day I see the paper. I read the paper every day cover to cover – I stay informed. And I see it. Picture of Sal and these two punks. And it hits me – those are the guys who jumped me! The story's about how they were robbing the mob, but the mob finds out and whacks them. They found the bodies in the Gowanus canal. So I gimp my way over to the bathroom and throw up. Sal set me up! Gets me shot to take the cash.

I'm pissed, and then I'm not because I can't stop thinking about his wife and kids. I'm numb for days and scared, because you just don't dump bodies in the Gowanus. That was a statement back when statements were still being made. Those bodies were meant to be found. A big warning to all the wannabes looking for upward mobility.

Things stay quiet. It's like the cops know but don't want to do anything because they don't want more blood on the street. Problem solved. Please go back to your programs. A capo comes into the club about a month later. Well dressed, big pinkie ring, bodyguard. Pulls me over and tells me I'm the new manager. I'm the new Sal. Don't fuck it up.

I'd like to tell you things go back to normal but they don't. The business slows down. The girls I get along with leave, and I'm sad to see them go. I know that's hard for you to understand. It was a just a job for all of us. We called the club "the office," kinda like that TV show. I always made sure they got treated right but it's hard when things are so bad. We don't need the velvet rope out front anymore because there's no more crowd. I even let the losers in because I can't go empty. More fights, more crap. It's like death by a thousand cuts, only it takes years. And the internet. Free porn on demand. It's killing us. I start thinking of opening an Irish bar on a beach somewhere. Florida? California?

But just when I think it's over, the Russians come to the rescue. And they got cash. Maybe the Virgin Mary came through for me after all. Instead of Tony and Paulie now we got Russian Yuri and all his friends lining up to get in just like the old days. And they bring in the Albanians who bring in the Turks who bring in the Egyptians. Instead of the cigarette machines, now we got hookas.

The business comes back. Not what it was but good enough. I get used to the silent treatment from my bosses. I do my job and we all make money so things settle down. The wiseguys know it's not my fault what happened when Sal had me shot so they're good with me. I even got Deirdre downstairs handling the girls. They start calling her "mom." My own mom passed from cancer and I promised I'd always take care of my little sister. As for me, I'm in Long Island. Me and Marisol. Bratty twins and a dog. I'm livin' the dream in Valley Stream.

Then one day Russian Yuri tells me he and his boys are buying the place. The mob's leaving the strip club game, and nailing Wall Street instead. A story for another day. He tells me he wants to cut me in on the real money. They don't want to waste time learning the business from the inside and they like me for the same reasons I was popular with la cosa nostra. They want to keep me tied down here and the only way they can do that is if I have skin in the game so they buy out the mob and I mortgage every blade of grass I own and go in with them.

We change the name to *Oasis* to give it an exotic feel. Yuri and his boys open more clubs in Brooklyn and even the city, and they want me keeping an eye on the books. So I'm a day guy now, driving the highway to work every morning with every other dope, rebuilding the great American strip club. At least I'm home for dinner so Marisol's happy. You gotta hand it to them, they're doing something right. The money's coming in fast and I'm running from club to club trying to keep up.

Still, I can't trust them. I get this feeling they're not being straight with me. They even fire Deirdre which is fine by her because she wants to spend more time with her kids, but it pisses me off. I start thinking about that bar on the beach again. Marisol wants me out of the business because she doesn't want me lying to the kids like Sal did with his. And I think about my own dad for the first time in years. I'm almost fifty now and maybe my time's short, like his was.

And then one day, the most perfect April day. I'm alone in the club doing the puzzle in the paper. All of the sudden the doors bust open. The FBI swarms in with Immigration right behind. They tear the place apart and put me in cuffs. Search warrants for all the clubs and my house. All the businesses shut down. My accounts frozen. Marisol cries every night, begging her family for money. They even interrogate Deirdre and her husband. It's like when I was shot – it's all happening so fast.

Turns out Yuri's boys would walk the streets of Moscow, find young girls and promise them an exciting life working at a fancy restaurant in New York City. Yuri gets them into the country and the next thing they know they're jammed into these tiny rooms in Sheepshead Bay, coming to work in vans, closely guarded. And Yuri's taking all their money. Only he was smart enough to put my name on everything and run back to Russia when he sensed the feds closing in. So I'm in it deep.

I never knew. Swear to God. I'm being legit here! I couldn't even talk to them, I don't speak Russian. They all seemed good every time I saw them. How could I know!?

I'm a wreck, impossible to be around. I tell Marisol to take the kids and go to her parents. She says maybe that's a good idea. I don't know if she believes me when I tell her my side. I go weeks without talking to anyone not even Deirdre. I'm lost thinking about these Russian girls. Where are they? Did they make it back home? Or did they disappear like that guy who ran over the mobster's son? The mafia has nothing on the Russians. They're just brutal. And then I'm thinking about all the other girls. What did we do to them? Who did I become?

I keep looking out the window waiting for someone to come around and throw me out of the house. My lawyer says I have to plead guilty and do jail time, no way around it. I swear to God I'm close to ending it all, thinking crazy thoughts. I get rid of the guns in the house just to be safe from myself. Somehow I just keep going. I just keep getting up. I do anything to stay positive, even try to remember a few prayers from when I was a kid. Me. Jimmy Murphy. St. Anne's High School Class of '89. Strip Club King of Queens. Human Trafficker. That's me now.

The other night I'm sleeping on a chair in my backyard because I can't take being alone in the house anymore. I have this dream. I'm on the beach and it's night. The sand is glowing this wild orange color. I see my parents. They're naked, standing in the water near the shore. There are these dark shadows moving around them that scare me. But then I feel it. I feel the love my parents had for me but never told me. The shadows vanish and there's this intense, bright feeling of love. I go to my parents. My mom kisses me on the cheek and my dad hugs me. The sun rises over the ocean. So gorgeous. And if it's the last good thing I ever see, I guess I can't complain.

# At Sea, Two Graces
# Jay Kelly

## 2nd Prize, Seán Ó Faoláin International Short Story Competition

You are five and a half months pregnant, just another young woman stealing away on the ferry to somewhere you might survive, to somewhere you might just have two things without being thought greedy or brazen: a place where you might even go to college and also keep your baby.

The Belfast port terminal is humid, dappled with travellers in the tumult of late afternoon. The commotion of other passengers evaporates into the muggy August air. You convey yourself and your brown leather case with the pink pompoms into the underbelly of the ferry. You feel the perspiration breaking out across your forehead; the inhaled engine fumes turn rancid in your stomach. When you finally reach the cafeteria level, the attendant checks your boarding card with theatrical slowness while you look across the open space, scouting out your seating options. By the time he gives you the nod and your ticket stub, you walk towards the quietest starboard seat. And though the ferry looks fresh, the wipe-clean seat smells of stale beer just the same.

At the table opposite, you recognise your mother's old neighbours, already drowsing, heads back and lips apart. Vera is nearest the window, still in her good travelling coat, and Mattie, brown as the shoes he mends for a living, has a faded Stewart's bag on his lap. And though you do not wish to be seen, you take the risk of sitting close by, because you have no energy left to seek out another spot.

The day before, you met him for the last time in the back bar of *The Northern Star.* You scanned the sides of the room, presuming he would sit somewhere discreet. Instead he was in the middle, just off reception, in a velvet armchair, a whiskey and ice in front of him, a bottle green tie, shimmering and loose at the neck. When the silence grew too ungainly, you smashed it. *I'm keeping it,* you said, looking well beyond him, to three panels of stained glass, beyond which everything was bevelled and yellow. His gaze fell to the floor then, like there was a challenging puzzle on the maroon and gold carpet, and he ran his fingers through his hair, like a child, with what seemed to be the wrong hand. *If it's a question of money,* he said, without looking up. A weight dropped then, from your chest through your body, like a slab of ice, his cold indifference in the heart of summer. *Don't worry about us, Tom, we'll be fine,* you said. He looked at you then, anger curling his brow, and said *You're kidding me?* You made no response. *Throwing yourself away, you are.* You looked toward the window and back to him. He seemed patient then, as if waiting for something habitual to occur: expecting his words to work. And you resolve not to give him that. And then you rose, presented the side of your face to him briefly, long enough to smell his smoky sweat, then let his Judas kiss settle on your cheek, like evidence.

The sea is unexpectedly rough. About a quarter of the way in to the crossing the cramps start, low and insistent. You go to the toilet several times, blaming the travel and the fried breakfast you had eight hours ago. On the fourth or fifth occasion, when you stand up to make your way back to the toilet, the room spins. You are dizzy and cold, but with a free arm, you wipe sweat from your face. The way to the toilet seems complicated this time, and you find yourself on a long white corridor where all the doors were closed. Maybe one is a toilet. You try a few but they don't open. You keep going and the ship lurches more and the cramps grow constant. The wall switches places with the ceiling and you are frozen. You think that maybe the Captain believes it is too hot and is funnelling cold air down the corridor at you. *Can you turn it off, please?* you say aloud. *Please. Please, someone, can you turn it off?* You look down and see a trail of blood red polka dots mottling the floor. You call out, *Help, please. Something is happening to someone.*

The next thing you remember is trying to turn in bed, but then you realise that you are not in bed, or even anywhere near home, and that your hands and feet are being held by four different men. *You're all right, love, we'll have you in the sick bay in no time,* says the nurse, a woman your mother's age, but slimmer, more mobile, standing tall and separate from them all. *I'm sure she's on her way over to be fixed anyway,* says the man holding your left ankle, his voice sounding flat and full of scorn. *Shut up out of that,* says another, *God love her.*

Once you reach the sick bay and they've laid you down on the bed, the nurse dismisses the men, then speaks to you quietly, *You're pregnant, lovey?* You nod and she takes your hand in hers, folds her warm fingers under your own. *Once upon a time I was a midwife in the Queen Mother's Hospital,* she says. Her hands are scrubbed raw, yet tender still. The sensation causes you to look up at her now and as you do, she brushes stray hairs from your clammy brow with her free hand. She leans in just closely enough for you to see the frankness in her slate-blue eyes. You know then how she sees that this is your baby and this is not a journey on which you ever intend to part with it. *Now listen to me,* she says, holding your fingers tight for emphasis, *there's nothing here but a lot of blood. No foetus.* You remember then, the words of the doctor in the health centre when you asked about the spotting and he said, with a voice full of venom, *if it's meant to stick, it'll stick.* And it is those words that for some reason you say aloud now, though in a different tone. *Don't talk like that, you we'en,* she says. Your body grows heavier on the bed, as if yielding to the kindness in her voice. *Is someone meeting you when you arrive?* Without waiting for an answer, she brings you a compress for your forehead, a basin of warm soapy water, a pack of oversized sanitary towels. After you clean yourself as best you can, she brings you a cup of well-sugared tea, pulls over a chair and says she'll stay with you for the rest of the crossing.

She can't know that you feel empty and tiny, like an infant yourself, but she stays with you just the same. And then she tells you stories, fabulous stories of babies born on the ferry, miraculous stories of babies rescued at sea, of the very first ultrasound machines in the world and how they were used right there in the centre of Glasgow, that you are arriving in one of the very best places in the world to have a baby, and then, as you draw close to the shore, she tells you the story of her own little girl, who is in fact around your own age, who has a child of her own and no husband and who lives in Aberdeen and who is, she says, hushing her voice now like she is about to reveal some enormous secret, *happy.* You dream of being her child now, and of your own child having a grandmother that could conceive of such things.

But then warm evening sun shines in through the porthole and, sitting up now on the thin metal-framed bed, you feel for one magnified moment like the sole recipient of the earth's tender attentions, and you realise then that there are things that you do have: the icy water she's just given you; a stomach that is no longer violently nauseous; a body that is certainly bleeding much less than before and this person, here with you now, with open ears, in front of whom you have permission to be, or even to speak, to pause to clear your throat and even to shriek, or cry or admit that no, no one will be there to meet you, that no one has ever really been there to meet you or mind you at all. And this silently granted permission to be, to speak or not to speak, releases something deep within you, some reservoir of life, some buoyancy on which you can float to shore, some knowing now that not only your baby, but *all* of this pain can somehow be borne.

When the ferry eventually pulls into Broomielaw and it is time to leave, she gives you her name, *Grace from Derby,* slips £5 into your hand, tells you to contact her if you need to. Then she writes her address and a note on the outside of an envelope in unexpectedly delicate cursive. It reads, *Get a taxi directly to Queen Mother Hospital,* then underneath, *Attention – Admissions Officer on Duty: Possible Placenta Praevia? Grace Bigsby, (Senior Midwife, Ret'd.).*

Yet somehow you do not need to contact her, because when you go there, even with no one by your side, even with a bare ring finger, a form with a blank under *Née,* and a tick beside *Father Unknown,* they admit you and scan you, just like she said, and they tell you that your placenta has grown low, has almost completely covered your cervix and that your job now is to avoid a catastrophic hemorrhage and what you must do, in fact all you must do, is lie in your bed, and almost nothing else at all. And so there you stay, save for very occasional slow circuits of the ward, growing plump on the hot, metal-lidded meals they bring you three times a day, for seventy-four luxurious days of compulsory idleness, until eventually they bring you, gowned and glorious and quivering with nervous anticipation, and almost exactly like every other woman on Prof. McCay's c-section list that day, to have your daughter's tiny, immaculate self, shucked clean from the centre of you. And three months later, when you leave the Special Care Baby Unit with her, yes, actually *with* her, you unfold the address in that envelope, and write just once, to say thank you, to let her know that Baby Grace has been born, early and perfect, and that she saved you both.

# The Book of Matthew
## Patrick Key

"Has it ever struck you that life is all memory, except for the one present moment that goes by you so quick you hardly catch it going?"

—Tennessee Williams

February 1985

I had been wrangled into a hunting trip to the family deer camp in Tuscaloosa County with my Dad, three uncles and their six friends. I had an intense resistance to the trip until I learned that my cousin Dewayne would be joining us with his dad. Albee was my dad's first cousin, which made Dewayne my 2nd. I never really understood the importance of cousin lineage, but Dad and Albee were the same age and grew up together and played football and were always close. It made sense to them that their sons had a natural connection too.

The deer camp was a large one room cabin that looked as if it had been built in the 1800s. It was set deep within a forest in West Alabama and perfect for prize deer hunting. My Dad and his brothers spent many weekends there during the winter months.

The cabin was completely wide open inside and smelled musty and dank. The sleeping quarters had two stacked rows of bunk beds around the edges of the wall, eight single beds per row. There was a small kitchen that had a working electric stove and a small refrigerator with a large silver handle like it was made in the 60's.

The center of the cabin featured an old-fashioned wood burning stove that had an aluminum chute rising out top of the stove that took the smoke out of the house. Rocking chairs had been positioned in a circle around the stove for conversation. Large, mounted deer heads had been unevenly hung around the space, their black glass eyes always watching, no matter where you were in the cabin. Towards the back wall was two giant shotgun racks with weapons of various sizes and shapes. A shelving unit next to the rack that held boxes of shotgun shells, some that were red cylindrical with a gold top, some green with a silver top, and some more dangerous looking bullets that were all gold and very slender, like a baby missile.

Albee and Dewayne picked us up on a Friday night in their green Jeep Wagoneer that had a removable hard white top. Dad, my Uncle Reece and Albee got in front and my cousin Dewayne said we'd ride in the back for the hour and a quarter drive to the camp. Dewayne let the tailgate down and I climbed in... a buffalo plaid print blanket laid out and a jam box with cassettes tapes to the right. He had a flashlight too and when he climbed in the back of the jeep, he laughed and pointed the spotlight on his bookbag pocket which had a pint of Mad Dog 20/20 Sloe Gin Fizz tucked in. He put his finger over his lips, raised his eyebrows and smiled to indicate a shared secret. He climbed in the back of the jeep beside me and pushed the sleeping bags up against the cab of the jeep and tapped the small window with a glimpse into the front indicating we were locked in and ready to go. He reached down and took a tape and put in the jam box, got the Mad Dog, and pressed play.

Prince's "I Would Die 4 You" started playing and I smiled knowing we had the same taste in music. He handed me the bottle of gin and said, "taste it, it's sweet." I hated the taste of alcohol, memories of being handed beer as a child flashing around my mind. I quickly took a drink and wanted to impress him with my like for it too, but my face was too revealing. "Keep drinking" he pushed, "it'll taste better soon," he said as we swapped drinks giving the bottle back and forth to each other, the fizzy red liquid leaving our lips a bright shade of raw. He was exaggerating the lyrics "I would die for you! HEY! I would die for you," and it made me laugh as we continued to drink.

It happened in a second, and I remember it so vividly. The click. My eyes blinked widely and seemed to stay open. I had an enhanced awareness, a warmth, an ease, a comfort, more laughs between us. The gin fizz was now taking full effect as it tickled my throat instead of making me gag. A long exhale of breath I'd sought for years all happened in an instant and I felt good.

As the jeep plowed over the bumpy road to the deer camp, the sloe gin fizz was working fast, we were talking and laughing. I remember leaning into him as we hit a hard turn, his hand falling on my leg above the knee. The jeep pulling over on the side of the road, all the men jumping out for quick relief, laughing and making fun of each other's stream. I was so shy, I never even attempted to go. When we arrived at the camp, the drive going by way too fast, I climbed out of the back of the jeep and lost my balance and fell over in laughter. We grabbed our things and stumbled inside the cabin, the other five men arrived earlier and had wasted no time getting the party started.

The rest of the night is hard to remember. I was elated and loose and I remember all the men were happy to see me so messy, masculine support, "he's drunk, he's drunk!" their encouragement making me feel like I belonged.

Hazy thoughts, lots of happy men in t-shirts and long johns, coonhounds and beagles running around the room looking for food and attention, whiskey and vodka and beer, talk of killing a buck the next day, hot women, and loud, hilarious laughter, so much laughter. I was both inside and outside myself at the same time. It was like watching a movie, but I was in the movie. The alcohol playing tricks on my mind. Hours seemed to pass slowly, then quickly.

It was late and I was in a chair by the fire watching as one by one, the others started passing out, like a poison had been placed in their drinks. I hadn't seen my Dad in hours which meant he likely went down first. I was hungry, but didn't want to eat, and the room was spinning slowly. The wood burning stove in the middle of the cabin providing minimal light and warmth to the entire room. Sitting in the rocking chair I was trying to gain my footing and finally it was quiet and dark, except for the company of the ever-curious deer heads on the wall. Getting sleepy, I glanced over at the long row of bunk beds full of snoring and farting men and trying to figure out where to collapse. I saw Dewayne raise his head ever so slightly, a sparkle in his dark brown eye indicating in silence that there was room for me in his bunk.

I looked around the room, no one was awake. I stumbled over.

The last light of ember on the fire seemed to give way to darkness.

I walked over and quietly climbed in the bunk, our bodies touching closely.

Overwhelmed and eager, I was afraid that all the men in the room would hear my heart beating.

I was dizzy with drink and my hand fell below his stomach; his intention was clear.

The room spinning faster, my heart beating stronger.

He gently grabbed my neck and turned my face and the front of my body away from him, my chin resting in the bent corner of his elbow, my head locked in place.

Unable to focus, I obliged. He softly placed his thick head of hair on my neck and with his other hand pulled down my underwear just enough.

His jaw moved, as if he was chewing, and then a spit, and then silence.

It was warm and wet and surprising and then without hesitation, his hand went over my mouth, and he held my neck back with the force of his forearm.

I wanted to scream when the fire hit my gut, but he squeezed my neck until I relaxed in his arm.

I was dizzy, in pain, scared, erect.

I finally gave up and leaned into the darkness and then I blacked out.

I woke up in a panic, with a gasp, not knowing where I was at first, but then the quick realization I was at the deer camp. The men were supposed to wake up before dawn to hunt and I had every intention of being a full participant as I felt I had something to prove to them. When I opened my eyes, I was still in Dewayne's bunk, the open room was empty, and quiet, a new fire was burning in the firepit, hints of daylight dotting the walls. My head hurt so bad, it felt like someone's boot was pressing down on the base of my skull, my eyes groggy with dried sleep, and I noticed my Dad was the only other person in the room. He was sitting in a rocking chair, with a bottle of whiskey in his hand, staring at me, slowly rocking back and forth.

I sleepily said, "where is everybody?" He didn't respond, just rocked.

After a minute, he got up and said, "let's get dressed, it's time to go hunt."

I climbed into the ill-fitting camouflage pants and put on a pair of yellow work boots that someone else had left at the hunting camp. I quickly ate a piece of Wonder bread on the counter and then I walked outside, and my Dad gave me a shotgun. "It's loaded, so hold the barrel down towards the ground," he commanded as we started our long walk into the woods. We must have walked for an hour, slowing down at times, pausing and squatting on the ground. The earth was wet, it had clearly rained the night before. My Dad still hadn't spoken to me which made me tense and I was sweaty and felt nauseous from last night's alcohol.

My Dad grabbed my shoulder and he pointed into the tree in front of us and we stopped. I squatted with him and saw the squirrel on the branch that grabbed his attention. He quietly and forcefully indicated it was time to shoot the defenseless creature and he showed me with his gun how to position my arms, so the rifle was aimed in the direction to kill.

He squinched an eye to show me how to see the vermin clearly through the view finder, and I mimicked his move. He nodded it was time. I released the safety, closed my eyes, and pulled the trigger. The kick of the gun pushing me back and the sound of the shot deafening me, leaving a constant ringing in my ear. After a moment, I opened my eyes and Dad was walking towards me with the dead animal in his hand. My eyes were blurry, and the squirrel looked so small in his large hand. As he moved towards me, he pulled out a large knife and sliced its furry tail off and stuffed it in my jacket pocket. The remains of the squirrels' body fell onto the wet leaves below. He grabbed me on the shoulder and patted me on the back and without any other emotion pointed with his finger the direction we should walk.

By the time we made it back to camp, the other eight men in the group were pulling up in their trucks and the excitement was palpable. The white top from the green jeep had been removed at some point and in the back where I'd been the night before on the buffalo print blanket, I saw Dewayne. He was holding the antlers of a giant 10-point buck he had just killed. A few of the men pulled the dead deer by his antlers to the edge of the tail gate, its front legs limp and open.

In an almost ceremonious act, Dad walked over and handed Dewayne the knife he had just used to slice off the tail of the squirrel. Using the large, serrated weapon, he quickly stabbed the chest of the deer and vigorously cut open the cavity. A quick flow of deep red blood started pouring everywhere on the truck and dripping to the ground. Dewayne forcefully reached in and grabbed the deer heart, violently ripped it out of the body and lifted it to the gods. As I was watching in awe and disgust, I suddenly remembered the night before, sharp flashes and images of pain, his warm alcohol laced breath, his thick hair on my neck. My heart felt like it stopped too and I felt sick again, like I was going to vomit.

I stood behind the other men who were celebrating, trying not to be noticed, keeping my eyes down as a million thoughts ran through my mind. I started to turn away to go inside and get far away from this ritual, but Dewayne said "hey, Matthew" a directive for me to stay, so I stopped in my tracks and looked over to him. The eyes of the other men now all looking in my direction. He dropped the muscle that only hours before had pumped life through the deer and jumped off the back of the tailgate and walked towards me.

He had a proud smile on his face and a vacantness in his eyes that reminded me of the eyes on the mounted deer heads inside. He reached his hand towards my jacket and pulled out the squirrel's tail that my Dad had tucked into the front pocket, he dangled it in front of my face then he let it drop on the ground. He then took his bloody hand and wiped it on my face, his finger marks leaving streaks of sinewy gore down my cheek onto my neck. He then grabbed my neck like he had done the night before and gave me a half hug and then a pat, and he turned back and walked towards the guys who were furiously shaking beer cans and opening them over him in a shower of adulation.

He joined the others as they pulled the jeep around the back of the cabin to string the deer up for cleaning and eventually cooking for supper. Before going inside, I bent down and picked up the squirrel's tail and put it back in my jacket pocket. A keepsake from the weekend.

# Exhibition of the Endlings
## Thomas Lawrance

You might have heard of the *Kauaʻi ʻōʻō* bird. You might even have heard the audio recording of the last *Kauaʻi ʻōʻō* bird, singing his mating call to a forest emptied of his kind. He leaves gaps where his partner should join in. It is an irreconcilable half-duet, with the bygone quality of some stray message beamed into outer space and forgotten about. Do not listen lightly.

I spent a long time listening to many such calls, as I swept up cigarette butts and crisp packets at the Exhibition of the Endlings. The Sumatran elephant was the loudest, standing on his island trumpeting to no one, a singular echo rolling out across the park and the planet. The booming voices of the Western and Eastern lowland gorillas would briefly trick visitors – and each other – but they were both male and had to be kept in separate enclosures. The tiny tree frog was our quietest resident. I would sometimes pause in the Amphibian House after hours and put my ear to the glass to hear her croak. When she died, nobody noticed for at least a week. Management liked to know the exact time and date that a species vanished forever, but the tree frog's disappearance was chalked up vaguely to 'February'.

We never had a *Kauaʻi ʻōʻō* – he was long gone by the time the Exhibition was founded – but our African grey parrot was a popular attraction. He was one of the few members of the collection who seemed to demonstrate an awareness of his situation. He came to us with half his feathers missing and a handful of curse words, and visitors could pay to hold and feed him. He seemed to enjoy the company, but in a sombre sort of way, as though he knew it was a pantomime imitation of a true life. His big eyes saw the facts of the Exhibition and his fruitless existence.

I spent most of my time at Maya's window. She had been rescued from a shack in Borneo, years after the official extinction of her kind. Her hair was shaved and her skinned scarred, but the keepers nursed her, and those great tufts of bright orange hair grew back in uneven patches. I always lingered as I cleaned the Orangutan House, because she liked to watch the repetitive motion of the brush, tracing it on the pane with her gigantic fingers. It was Maya I worried about first – before even myself – when the tiger got out.

12:38pm, 12th April – Arctic fox.

12:47pm, 12th April – red panda.

12:51pm, 12th April – Bengal tiger.

They had to shoot him before he reached the primates. They say the rifleman wept as he fired, and resigned that same day.

The incident – and the associated loss of three valuable exhibits – threatened everything. The crowds thinned. There were entire contingents who would only come to see the red panda or the tiger, and we lost them overnight. Funds trickled away. A new management team was brought in. They held several meetings, and the red squiggly lines on their graphs all pointed down. Money was saved where possible – the restaurant was downgraded, and half the toilet facilities were scrapped – but it wasn't enough.

I was washing Maya's windows (she imitated my movements with a fistful of leaves) when one of my staff, Carla, brought me a rumour: management were holding an auction. I stormed up to head office to make my opposition known, but I was quietly informed that the process had already begun. The smaller exhibits were being sold off to save the larger ones. The axolotl had gone to a Russian oligarch, and the grey parrot was being shipped at that very moment to an actor's penthouse in Los Angeles. A flurry of publicity soon accompanied each sale – the last pangolin received her own reality TV series (the second series introduced a co-star, the last sloth).

As head cleaner, I was familiar with all of these exhibits, no matter how tiny, and I was horrified to see them lifted from their habitats – artificial as they were – and delivered to paying customers. The Belalanda chameleon succumbed to stress, and was gone before they could pack him off to Beijing (9:27am, 8th September). Soon, the smallest endling in the park was the Fennec fox. She was old and diseased, unfit for sale – but expensive. She vanished from her enclosure one night. I don't know what happened to her, but her disappearance saved several hundred dollars a month.

After the sale of fourteen exhibits and the disappearance of the fox, the auctioning stopped. The practice was deeply unpopular with the staff. Carla and I marched into the office every time another sale was announced on the news – and we would announce our refusal to clean a part of the park. We'd match every sale with another facility. Soon we had abandoned all the toilets, and, by the time the sloth went, the bins were overflowing.

Management relented, and – instead of selling off any more exhibits – the decision was made that the park would begin to offer travelling shows. Endlings would be taken to schools and colleges, displayed for paying guests in educational lectures. I was still unhappy to see the bonobo and the snow leopard crammed into crates and carted offsite, but at least they were returned in the evenings. Mops dutifully in hand, Carla and I offered to accompany the travelling shows, but we were told that all cleaning staff were to remain at the park. I stuck even closer to Maya at this time. Recently she had begun to mirror my actions with the sweeping brush, carefully brandishing a branch and scraping it along the floor in tandem. I remember learning about the Neanderthal people as a child, and being fascinated that an animal with all the brains and wit and feeling of a human being could ever disappear. Now, gazing into Maya's scratched brown eyes, it didn't strike me as fascinating. It was mundane. Maya sat on her concrete floor tossing strands of hay about, idly watching as I filled buckets and scrubbed the information signs. Pongo pygmaeus, once native to the rainforests that used to cover Borneo. The more intelligent endlings, like Maya, were obviously conscious of the park's changes. She retreated into the shadows whenever the tranquilised Western and Eastern gorillas were wheeled past her window, on their way to some offsite exhibition.

The spider monkey failed to return from one such trip. We were told that he had died from some undiagnosed condition, but his body was not brought back for burial in the memorial garden, as was standard procedure. The same thing happened a few weeks later when the chimpanzee's cage came back empty.

I had just given my team their relaxed instructions for the day (there was much less to do now) when I saw a particularly large crate being lifted onto one of the travelling exhibition trucks. I accompanied Carla to clean the elephant's shed and then went on my own to shine Maya's windows – I liked to make sure that she could see clearly, as her enclosure afforded her a view over the black rhino's paddock. I had been scrubbing for twenty minutes, expecting Maya to emerge from her sleeping quarters, when I realised that her gate was unlocked. Hay was scattered about outside, and I clocked – far too late, shamefully late – that she must have been taken away.

I went straight to the office, demanding to know where Maya was.

'She's being used in a lecture on hominid morphology.'

'Which college?'

'You weren't so concerned when the gorillas were taken out – and they're safely back in their enclosures. Which, if I'm not mistaken, are yet to receive today's cleaning.'

I trudged to my duties, but kept an eye on Maya's home for the rest of my shift. Our hours had all been cut, and I had to leave early, but I went straight to her window in the morning.

Maya was still absent.

'What happened?'

'I'm sorry, but the orangutan passed away. Heart failure. We should have diagnosed it earlier. I need you to wash down her enclosure so that we can put the bonobo in there.' He gestured vaguely to the plans on the wall, which displayed management's intentions to shrink the park and sell the excess land to developers. 'Can you get on with that, please? We can't afford to delay.'

From then on, I fulfilled my duties with a long overdue dejection. The park was quieter. Since the day of the tiger's escape, the elephant's behaviour had decayed even further, and now he made no sound at all. At the beginning, he would react to our presence in his enclosure, sometimes defensive, sometimes curious, but now he didn't see us at all. I couldn't be entirely sure that he wasn't blind. He just faced the walls. My days were shorter, and the enclosures fewer. In place of the elephant's call and the cry of the spider monkey, we could hear the drills and diggers of the developers over the fence. I cleared the orangutan's enclosure as instructed, but I didn't remove the information panel. I only covered it with the bonobo's, so that it would still be there – some small, flat trace of Maya in the park.

It was six months before I learned that she had not died. I was tidying the management offices, dusting a neglected side-room with faded wildlife protection posters on the walls. In the gloom I knocked over an old wastepaper bin, spilling a year of crumpled sheets onto the sticky tiled carpet. A bright yellow ball of carbon paper caught my eye, and I smoothed it out on the desk. It bore the traces of a sales receipt. Handwritten. Pongo pygmaeus. Dated the day Maya disappeared.

'What's this?'

He saw no point in lying. 'It's a sales receipt for the orangutan.'

'Who took her?'

'Businessmen.'

'Where did they take her?'

'I don't know. They said Riyadh, but...' He shrugged.

'Is this what happened to the rest?'

'Yes. Well, the chimpanzee, actually, he did die – but the others, yes.'

'This is outrageous.'

'We're trying to save money here.'

'No, you're trying to make it.'

He looked at me. 'We're cutting costs.'

Two days later, my entire cleaning staff was dismissed, cast out into the wilderness. Some left the country in pursuit of increasingly elusive jobs, some became homeless, some I never heard of again. Too late we noticed the correlation between extinctions and geopolitical crises. When we lost the sharks, we lost the fishing industry; when we lost the fishing industry, we lost entire countries.

'Please, do something.' It was the last thing Carla said to me. I never found out where she went.

Of course it's occurred to me, in the years since, that I could've downed my tools. I know that. I could've demanded my staff back, gone on a solo strike. But you must understand, it would only have resulted in my own prompt dismissal. Work is hard to find, so I clung to my job like a sickness. I kept my head down after that, and didn't lift it for ten years.

When I did, the only endlings left were the elephant – who had assumed the aspect of concrete, fused to his surroundings – and the Galápagos giant tortoise. I'd forgotten about the tortoise. I think everyone had. He was so slow and silent as to be invisible, and he'd avoided the public auctions and the secret sales. He was lucky. When Darwin and his crew sailed home in 1836, they ate all their tortoises. According to the sign outside his pen – thick with the grime I'd neglected to wipe – our giant tortoise was 174 years old. He looked every second of it.

I was at home when I heard. I rushed to the park, fuelled by some fantasy that I could do something, but the flames were visible five miles away.

Our facilities were good, once, when we started. Not perfect. We had no marine capacity. One of the early locator teams, searching the Yangtze riverbanks for surviving Chinese alligators, spotted the last baiji dolphin from their boat. It circled them for a while, playing in the brown waves. When evening came, they had no choice but to watch it disappear into the murk. They returned without the alligator.

The Exhibition burned all night. They never got the culprit. We are left without motive. The police suggested that it might have been an act of revenge by one of the many sacked. Others point to insurance fraud. Fewer generously say accident, or mercy-killing, or some natural recapitulation of the fires that wiped out the last of the rainforests. Nobody asked me, but I know it's simpler than all that. I knew that place and the people there, and I realised, as I swept up the ashes on my last job, that whoever burned down the Exhibition of the Endlings, consigning those last two pitiful specimens to history, was simply a completist.

# Down the Old Road

## Kate Norris

I live off the small road. You know the one where you go out past the cathedral and down by the graveyard and you keep going until the road gets narrower and narrower and there's only room for one car and you can't see round the bend? Well, I live down there. I have to walk home from school most days and it's over two miles. Or that's how far Mam told me it was. I'm not really good at knowing distances but it takes me about forty minutes to walk from the school gate to the front door. When we leave school we have to line up at the gate with Sister Josephine, she has short grey hair and brown teeth from all the tea she drinks and she hits us with a ruler whenever we don't have our homework done. I've never been hit with the ruler but one day she made me stand on the chair in the classroom because I was talking too much.

I know the way home by heart but sometimes I walk it before I go to sleep just to check, so I never get lost when I'm walking it on my own. You go down past the convent where they keep the nuns at night and cross over safely at the traffic lights, make sure you wait for the green man and look left and right before you cross, otherwise you might get killed. After those lights you can skip and run all the way to the big church because you don't have to cross again and you don't have to walk on the road yet. My favourite part is before the graveyard, there's an old stone house covered in climbing plants that you can barely see and there's a small field beside it with a stone wall that also looks very old. If I stand on my tippy-toes, I can see horses in the field. There's usually one horse in it but she had a baby and now he's with her. I go all the way to the secret house with its secret garden to look at Chestnut and Acorn, that's what I named them. Last week they came over to me when I was standing there and put their heads close to mine and I was able to pet their noses. Acorn was a bit shy so I only petted him once because sometimes I'm shy too and I don't like it when people try to touch me, so I understood. Chestnut has brown coarse hair and big sad eyes, Acorn is the same colour but softer with a white stripe down his nose, his eyes aren't as sad but the field is a lot bigger to him and he hasn't explored all of it yet. After the horses the scary part happens where I have to go past the graveyard. I don't know anyone there apart from a girl who used to be in my school. She was a bit older than me and she always used to get hit with the ruler. One day she was at home and she fell down the stairs and she hit her head so badly that she died. After that, Mam told me to make sure I go down the stairs really carefully. Sometimes I talk to the people in the graves and I read their names and dates of birth and dates of death and I count how old they were when they died. Some of them were really old and died not so long ago and other ones were eight or nine like me and died a long time ago. You know when the last time they were visited was by how dead the flowers are. When we drive past the graveyard at night I can see little red and white lights flickering and floating in the dark that I don't see during the day. I think it's the souls of all the dead people trying to get out of their graves but maybe not because they must all be in heaven. I pray every night to God out of the window for their souls just in case. I don't say the Rosary or the Our Father but I make up my own prayers and I think that should be all right with God.

Other days I run, run, run as fast as I can so I don't have to look at the headstones. On days like that I don't even care if I step in the muddy puddles and splash dirt and mud all up the backs of my white socks and sometimes even onto the back of my skirt. Those are the days that I keep my hand sticking out into the shrubs and I can see how many blades of grass I collect. After I've run till I have no breath left inside me at all I count them and pull them apart one by one. Or I make a slit in the middle of one and blow through it to make a whistling sound.

Next, there's the fireplace building company and the turkey farm. The turkey farm smells so bad that I have to hold my breath for 20 seconds which is okay. I've been practicing in the bath on Sunday nights before school. I hold my nose and slide under the water keeping my eyes closed so as not to get soap in them and I count for as long as possible until the bubbles start spilling out and I have to stop. Ninety-seven. That's my record. I never hear the turkeys in their farm, probably because I'm running so fast. After the fireplace-makers there's a strange house that has a tin roof. I know from history class that lots of people used to live in cottages with roofs made of straw but that was years and years and years ago. Jimmy, the taxi man, and his wife Maura, who works in the chippy, live there. Jimmy dropped us into town once after he saw us walking and he wouldn't take any money from Mam when she tried to pay him. We never got in his taxi again after that because we're not charity cases.

After that comes all the Treanor houses. There's Helen Treanor with a thick orange face, a sheen of rose lipstick and a dog. I have to look for a stick in the bushes before I walk past her house because of that dog. He's not a very big dog, I think he's a spaniel but he likes to run out of the garden and nip at your ankles. Maybe his bark is worse than his bite but I don't want to find out. I don't hit him with the stick, it's just for protection. The stick is also good for poking around in the well. It's a secret well in the ditch that I like to look in before I get chased by the dog. There's a little trickle of water that falls into it and you can see your reflection in it. I stir the stick in the water and pull out little flowers and see how deep the well is by measuring how far the water goes up the stick. It never goes more than halfway up. Which means I won't drown if I fall in. If I have coins in my pocket I throw the brown ones in and make wishes. I can count my wishes in one and two penny coins.

Helen Treanor doesn't care that her dog chases me, she never ties him up and always leaves the gate open. Which I think is a very un-neighbourly thing to do. The next Treanor house belongs to Long John Treanor, he doesn't need to keep his gates closed because his dog Flo is very old. She doesn't bark very loud and she doesn't run very fast. She doesn't actually run at all. I think she must be a great-great-grandmother now. Long John has a big, booming laugh and I only come up to his waist when I stand up straight as I can. He calls me Rosie because he doesn't know my name, he calls all the girl children Rosie and all the boy children Toby.

When I walk past the gates Long John invites me in and lets me say hi to Flo. He gives me hard boiled sweets that taste like oranges. They're not my favourite but you never say no to free sweets, unless they're being offered by a stranger. Flo had puppies last year, I never even noticed how big she was until they were already born, all eight of them, little black balls of fluff rolling around her, grabbing at her nipples for milk. I had to look away but I could see that two of them were tiny, smaller than the rest, and they couldn't get any milk. I told Mam about them and she went to see Long John and ask about the puppies. When we got there the puppies were nowhere to be seen and he was carrying a big, brown, wriggling sack. My heart started to beat really fast and I heard Mam shouting stop, stop, that he couldn't do it, that he was cruel and heartless. He wasn't happy but she managed to get him to give her two of the pups, the two runts of the litter. Our house was too small for me, Mam and eight puppies anyway. We called them Georgie and Pauline but they were so sick and they couldn't eat anything so after three days they died and we had to bury them at the back of the garden. I didn't understand why they had to die but Mam told me it was God's will, God has to make difficult decisions about who stays on Earth and who goes to Heaven, like he did with Dad. I prayed to God that night and I asked him why they couldn't stay with us but he never told me. God is very quiet.

The road forks after all the little houses and there are less and less cars going past so I take the right lane and I can walk in the middle of the road, I just have to make sure I stand in close if a car does come. You can't see around the bends so you have to keep your ears listening carefully. The road isn't new on the way to my house and little tufts of grass grow up in the middle of it. I don't know how anyone could even try to cut them. The bushes grow bigger and the trees try to touch each other when they're reaching for the sky and put shadows all over the ground that I make sure I don't step on. It gets really quiet and I can hear every rustle in the leaves.

I pray to God then as well, well it's not really praying because I don't say "Dear God" at the beginning like I do at night-time, but that's when I talk to him the most. Sister Josephine says that you have to go to confession and go to Mass to be close to God but Mam says God is everywhere, in the fields, in the air, all around us. Which makes sense when you think about how God made everything. He made it all in six days which is amazingly fast and he did it all by himself. When I speak to him on the way home it's not about anything important, just little things. I used to ask him for stuff but I stopped doing that. God has to listen to millions of people asking him for stuff every single day so I don't think he needs me to do it as well. I talk about school and friends and all the things that have happened. I talk to him about Mam and how she cries at night in the kitchen when she thinks I'm asleep. I've seen her at the table when I go in after a bad dream and her face is wet and shiny and she wipes it before she kisses me goodnight. She doesn't cry during the day, only I do that, and all I need is a kiss to make it better.

All the quiet and all the bends later, and I'm almost at our gates. There's only one house beside ours and they don't have any grown-up children like me, only a baby. Mam says they're newly-weds and they live in a house with two storeys not one so they can put more babies in the rooms in the future. It makes me sad they'll be too small for me to play with by the time they're here. I used to wish I had a sister to play with but I don't think that's going to happen anymore. Mam told me I was going to have one when I was six and I was so excited that I planned everything we'd do together, how I'd do her hair all pretty when it had grown long enough, how we'd play in the stream beside the field and race leaves under the bridge, how we'd learn songs to dance to together and how we'd tell each other secrets in the night-time before we fell asleep. I remember that it was around Christmas time, maybe after Christmas because I had my new Sindy doll and there was still snow outside and it was very, very dark. I heard sounds coming from the bathroom and went to investigate. When I got to the door I realised that it was Mam making the noises and I called for her. She shouted at me not to come in but I pushed the door open anyway because I was scared she was hurt. She was lying close to the toilet on the floor.

Her face was all wet and there were splashes of blood all around her and in one pool of blood I saw something, something small and hard looking. Mam moved her foot and I couldn't see it any more, all I could see were the smudges of blood. She wiped the floor and her face and sent me back to bed. In the morning she made my favourite breakfast, pancakes with butter and sugar.

The gates to our house are old and rusty and the driveway is long with lots of weeds. We used to have three big fir trees running along the garden but there was a big thunderstorm one night and the lightning hit one of the trees so now we only have two. They're my favourite climbing trees and they're also good to sit under because they keep you dry whenever it's raining, which is all the time where we live. I know I'm home when I see the treetops. That's when I know that Mam will be waiting for me to come in the door and she'll make us both a cup of tea. Mine will be extra milky with half a sugar and hers will be extra strong and extra sweet. I'll do my homework at the table while she boils potatoes for dinner. If I'm really good, she'll let me stay up late and I'll be allowed to sit on the settee and watch a film with her until I'm sleepy and then she'll carry me to bed. After she's gone, I look out of the window and sometimes see the moon almost touching the tops of the trees, casting its pale light over the winding, narrow road I know by heart. Other nights, I see only stars. That's when I close my eyes ever so tight and make my bedtime wish. I'd tell you what I wish for, but then it wouldn't come true.

# Farming Prices

## Eimear O'Callaghan

It won't be long now. Heather wedges a thumb behind the lump of elastic she's sewn into the waistband and itches the angry welt in her side. She thought she'd have gone early with this one. God knows, she's done more than her fair share of pushing and panting in the past eight years and she's more than ready. But no. Like the snow that's been falling and thawing and freezing since Christmas, and falling all over again, this pregnancy feels like it's going on forever.

The washing machine belches hot water and steam. Condensation weeps from the ceiling, and drips down the green walls. It seeps into the cracks on the windowsill, where greasy black mould will soon fester again. Heather leans against the stove, away from the suds that are bubbling and sloshing onto the lino. She looks down at the puffiness slumped around her ankles. Pregnancy has given her an old woman's legs.

'It's a present for you. A surprise,' William had told her when the shiny Hoovermatic was unloaded at the top of the laneway, one morning in July. He'd bought it in Magherafelt on the never-never after she told him 'number six' was on the way.

But he's a good man. He means well.

She wipes the fogged-up window and places her hand on her blazing cheeks, savouring its delicious coolness. Apart from dark bitter branches of hawthorn that even the snow won't stick to, there's nothing to see but white. The cattle and sheep were moved weeks ago. Nothing stirs, not even a bird. Nothing has stirred for days, or maybe weeks. She barely knows what day it is anymore.

'That's a quare job,' he says, cocking his head towards the twin-tub. He presses himself against her as he squeezes past for his wellingtons and she tries to shrink herself.

Never mind that we can't afford the damned thing, she wants to say.

*'For your heavenly Father knoweth that ye have need of all these things,'* he says, reading her as always. 'Matthew, 6:32.'

'Aye,' she says. 'A godsend.'

A blue rubber hose chunders grimy water into the sink. One of the twins is calling from the hallway, battling to be heard above the machine. Heather longs to take off her shoes, to stand in her stocking feet, but the floor's too wet.

Maybe she'll step outside and lie down. Spread out her arms and legs, fill her lungs with the air blowing in from Russia and sleep the sleep of the dead. Let the snow pile up and over her. One or other of the two brothers would find her.

The washing machine shudders to a pause and a sigh of silence washes over her, hauling her back to the now.

This snow can do strange things to a head.

'Tell Robert there's soup and spuds if he wants them,' she calls.

Living like this could make her mad.

William, in the hallway, doesn't answer. Maybe he hasn't heard her. Maybe he has. It doesn't matter. Robert won't call in.

The broth smells of the onions and carrots they'd put by, warm and earthy, and it cuts through the soapy steam. She lowers the blue flame. No lumps of shin beef or mutton these days but it will warm them when they stumble in later with their faces scorched by the cold, their socks and mittens sodden.

It's the worst winter in Ulster for two hundred years, according to the Belfast Telegraph. That was when the papers could still get through. Everywhere is blanketed, six feet deep in places, and higher in the drifts. Cars and buses lie exhausted and abandoned. William's work at the quarry has stopped.

The youngsters' hats and gloves smell of scorched wool when she gathers them from the hearth and presses them to her face. The nappies, too, are dry now, stiff and creased with the grid of the fireguard. The room doesn't hold any heat and she wipes away the film of moisture that clouds the face of the mantel clock. Cold seeps in around window- and door-frames that are warped by years of damp.

'Right, you lot,' William calls, and she allows herself to breathe. Lizzy and the boys dance around him. Sarah bawls to go out too. A piercing rawness surges through the cottage when William unbolts the front door. Robert will be down in his tractor to help clear the laneway and dig them out.

A pain judders across Heather's lower back as she plunges the long wooden tongs into the suds and hauls out the steaming clothes. Perspiration beads her forehead. This child will come before morning. The spin drier squeals and screeches as it gathers speed, wakening the baby from his nap.

Heather lets the doorframe take her weight as steam gushes out around her and escapes into a silvery sky. Goosepimples tingle her arms and legs, and her breath glistens white on the sharp clear air. Hunching up her shoulders, she shudders to life. She cups a hand beneath her belly's drag and moulds the round hardness of the baby.

Slieve Gallion lurks behind a veil of frozen mist and the sky hangs low. On clear days, she can look across the fields and follow Robert's red Massey Ferguson trundling down from the farmhouse. There's been talk, William told her, of couples dancing and skating on the lough over there. 'As sure as there's an eye in a goat,' he'd said, shaking his head, 'some character from the lough-shore drove his Mini across it.'

Up here, they could be the only ones left in the world. A family trapped in a gigantic snow globe.

Robert hasn't crossed their door in months. Today will be no different. He stopped in the tractor at the end of the lane a few times when William was working in the bottom field. That was before the snow came. Heather had watched them from the house, envying their easy conversations.

William didn't say what they talked about nor remark on Robert and his wife not visiting anymore. But that's the way he is. Heather doesn't mention it either.

*********

All Heather had ever wanted was someone to take her away from the town and the Imperial's daily grind. Someone to put a roof over her head and give her a home and a squad of children. A man she'd grow to love and who might love her back. Someone different to her father.

The Wilsons' father, also Robert, had been dead less than a year when William brought her home to meet his mother. It was a dreary Ulster Sunday. Cloud weighed down on Slieve Gallion and November rain lashed the farmhouse windows. Net curtains, drawn tight, filtered the sparse daylight.

Elizabeth had a table laid squarely for tea and waited for them by the open fire with a prayer book on her lap. In a silver-grey cardigan, and a black pleated skirt that skimmed her ankles, she wore her widowhood with pride. A small cameo brooch was pinned at the neck of her blouse.

The conversation strained over roast beef sandwiches and homemade boiled fruit cake. The brothers chose to eat rather than talk much.

Elizabeth quizzed Heather about working at the Imperial and living in the town. There was little to bring the likes of her to that side of the hill, she said, having tried in vain to place Heather's wretched family in the County Londonderry landscape.

'It's only one of the cows,' Robert said, when a succession of plaintive high-pitched roars drifted through one of the many silences.

The wet air was heavy with the smell of dung when William and Robert guided her along the waterlogged track to the yard. Elizabeth had suggested she should change out of her shoes. There was nothing she could do about Heather's green plaid dress with its tiny nipped-in waist and white Peter Pan collar, the one she kept for Sundays.

Heather's feet slapped about in a pair of William's rubber boots as she tramped through the mire with the brothers. Her fear of losing her footing matched her fear of losing these men, and she linked arms with them both. She'd happily have settled for either.

Rain rattled off the corrugated iron roof of the shed where the cattle shuffled and snorted, colliding against each other with dull thuds. Steam rose off their backs and vanished into the cold musty air. Drawn towards the mournful sound, Heather walked on ahead through the murk.

The cow stood apart from the others, her red-brown coat wet and matted. She stretched her head high and bellowed, a steady and high-pitched cry. Distress gleamed in her huge wet eyes. William put an arm around Heather's waist and reached across the rails to pat the animal's broad head.

'Ssh there, girl. Easy. Ssh.'

As they trudged through the muck and puddles, on their way back to the farmhouse, Heather welcomed the warmth and security of William's hand. Thirty acres in the Sperrins could never provide for both Robert and him, he told her, and whatever children they and their wives might be blessed with. But if she married him, the cottage at the edge of the farm could be theirs.

Life is so random, Heather thinks yet again, as she breathes on the misted window and watches the two brothers in the laneway below, digging and scraping, scooping and bending. Another ache passes through her. She digs her fists into the fleshy softness above her hips.

It was another waitress – a girl she barely knew – who'd coaxed her to go to a Young Farmers' dance in Dungiven. She'd have danced anywhere in those days.

If she'd gone to the local Hall as usual that night. If the band had finished with another slow set, or if they'd played another Ladies' Choice. If Robert instead of William had asked that night to see her again.

Their silhouettes against the whiteness are so different. Robert, low-set and broad, casts shovelfuls of snow in sweeping arcs that are smooth and graceful.

William digs quickly. He switches between stretches of the laneway while watching the youngsters and showering them with snow when they scamper into his range. With his long, lanky limbs, he moves as quickly as they do. She remembers his dancing, his two left feet.

She'd only ever meant it as fun but in bed in the early years, she'd tease him that she could have married Robert instead. He was a better dancer by far. And William would play along, urging her to imagine what she might've got up to with his older brother instead.

It was different now. There's no music to waltz away her thoughts, in the small dark hours when the walls, the ceilings and Slieve Gallion closed in on her. William would turn away and his breathing would tell her he wasn't asleep. He'd whisper that she'd have been better off with Robert and she'd tell him to stop talking like that. She'd hug him. He was a better man than the likes of her ever had a right to hope for.

She should remind him that he'd done her a favour. That at twenty-five she'd almost despaired of finding a good man but she'd say nothing. She was fond enough of him now not to cause him any hurt. She'd never admit that, he or his brother, it wouldn't have made any difference to her. She'd have been grateful for either of them.

'As capable a woman as he'll ever find,' Elizabeth had said, when Robert announced he was marrying Judith, a few months after William and Heather's wedding. Judith's family farmed locally and worshipped at the same church as the Wilsons. When Elizabeth died three years later, she was content that her eldest had married a good woman. The farmhouse was in competent hands.

'Do you think Robert's happy?' Heather had asked William one night.

'I can't see why he wouldn't be,' he said. His tone told her the conversation was going no further. He didn't inquire why she asked. He left her no reason to tell him that Robert used to visit her before the summer.

The pains are spreading beneath and through her belly now, on down into her thighs. If she can get the youngsters rounded up, there'll be time to have them fed and settled before the baby comes.

Heather stands in the doorway calling but her words freeze and splinter in the cold. Lizzy and the boys, flashes of blue, red and green, pretend not to see her as they slide and skate on the compacted snow gleaming in the watery sunshine.

The gold and purple crocuses she planted will be burrowing through the frozen soil, the snowdrops almost ready to thrust their heads upwards with the final thaw.

William stands up to stretch and notices her.

When the contractions subsume her later and the youngsters are deep in sleep, he kisses the top of her head. He leaves her to the midwife and goes to the front room to pray.

*********

The boy comes easily in the end. Heather basks in the tranquility of those first few hours, alone with her baby before the world stakes its claims. His scrunched-up fists, the Wilson cleft in his tiny chin. She watches for the instant when his eyelids flash wide and he stares with eyes as dark as night.

This one will give them no bother. Another gentle soul who'll leave them one day like they all will, boarding the bus to the city or taking the Liverpool boat. Maybe he'll go to America.

There's nothing for them here on the mountain.

William pokes the fire on the other side of the wall, breaking up the embers to tease them back to life. She hears the clump of new clods of turf, then the hiss of wet slack that will keep the fire in until daybreak. The fireguard clinks as he drags it across the hearth.

'Shout if you want anything,' William tells her, placing a hot water bottle beneath her feet. A smell of soot wafts from his hands as he moves the Wilson family's Moses basket closer to the side of the bed.

Heather doesn't know how long she's been dozing when something, other than the coldness, unsettles her. She reaches out in the half-light for the crib. The infant's cheek is warm and soft to her touch. Oblivious to the harshness beyond, he sleeps as though he's still nestled in her womb. A two-bar electric fire glows in the corner but its heat expires before reaching them.

Heather's hair is plastered against her neck. The pillow, still damp with her sweat, is clammy and cold against her shoulders. As her eyes adjust to the dimness, shapes become more solid, their edges sharper. She senses William's presence before turning to see him, a dark form in front of the curtains with his back to her.

'I didn't know you were up.'

The hands on the alarm clock glow luminous green. Almost six o'clock. She's been sleeping for more than an hour.

Heather pulls the candlewick bedspread around her shoulders as the infant's whimpering turns to a high-pitched mewl. His tiny mouth searches for her nipple and she tucks the cover under him, sealing him tight to her body.

'Has the snow stopped yet?

William must have dressed in the dark. He's fully clothed, wearing the heavy jacket he wore all day in the snow.

He speaks, says something to her. She can't have heard him properly. Her heart is racing, the pulse pounding in her ears.

'Did you hear what I said?' he asks, still facing into the curtains.

There's a tightening in her chest and she struggles to get enough air. Like those long dark nights when she moved here first. The crazy terror when something moved in the shadows or made a sound behind her, when she wanted to run and scream but couldn't. The same fear takes hold of her now. She stares at her husband's back.

She has heard him properly.

William draws the curtains apart and grey-blue light floods the room. Pools of water gleam on the lino. Lumps of snow slither off his black rubber boots.

He turns around to face her and the snowlight intensifies the blackness beneath his eyes, the eerie pallor of his cheeks.

'Judith has everything ready,' he says. 'A cot, bottles, nappies, the lot.'

Heather tries to swallow, rapid gulps of air. Her voice is locked in her throat.

She curls her hand around the baby's down-covered head and as cramps grip her stomach, blood gushes warm between her legs.

A strangled giggle escapes from her mouth.

'I don't know what you're talking about,' she says, her voice tight and pinched.

William approaches the bed, bringing with him the bitter reek of the winter countryside. He fixes his eyes on the wall above her head. A twitch above his left nostril belies his usual calm.

'They've been trying, Heather. You know that as well as I do.'

'No.'

'Robert needs a son. He always has done. The farm needs a boy.'

Heather feels like her heart will burst.

'They're not taking my baby.'

'Five thousand pounds. That's what he's giving us.' His voice is louder and more confident now. 'Or maybe you'd rather some jumped up fenian got the farm when he goes. Is that what you want?'

No words come out of her. And suddenly she understands. She sees them at the bottom of the lane. The brothers deep in conversation when she imagined they were talking about football. Or politics. Or the price of land. The price of beasts at the market.

'We need the money,' William says. 'We don't need another one of these.'

His eyes move to his son for the first time since the midwife had called him in.

'My son. Robert's son. What's the difference?' he says, almost in a whisper. 'We'll get it over with before the thaw comes. At least this one will get a chance.'

As the violet dawn gives way to a slate-grey sky, William stands outside the cottage to wait. A filigree of frost adorns the bedroom window, whorls and ferns that cloud Heather's view of the laneway. She breathes on the glass and watches them disappear, the way the tracks that Robert's car will leave will vanish beneath the next fall of snow.

The child continues sleeping in the Wilson family's crib as, in ever-widening circles, Heather scrapes away more patterns with her fingernail. The powdery crystals scatter and vanish. She presses her icy fingers on the hot hardness of her breasts, growing tender from her milk coming in. She stares through the mist at where the mountain should be.

The heart-rending cry that had rent the gloom. She, in her best green dress and only winter coat, going home that Sunday splattered with mud. The pitiful beast, its breath steaming from its nostrils, its flanks heaving with every bellow.

She recalls how William had patted the dumb animal's head.

'She's crying for her calf. That's all,' Robert had said, before leaving Heather in the sheds with William.

'He took it from her yesterday,' William had told her. 'Don't worry about her. She'll go on like that for a day or two but she'll get over it. They always do.'

## The Curse

Breda Spaight

My father slathers the vulva
with lubricant, the fat lips glossy
as a chestnut, while my brother holds the tail
from which clinkers of dried shit dangle,
her ginger flank also matted in shit. She stands
in the cattle crush, head clamped in the bail,
looking like a tourist admiring the view
through the open window of a train, as though
her head has nothing to do with her body
and her body is all about what she carries,
as my father grasps and grapples with the slithery, banana
-yellow hooves spreading the vulva, as only the vulva can
spread, flap to the world girdled in fibres spun to burn;
my brother holding the tail's butt now, raising it up as my father
nooses the calf's legs with ropes, first one, then the other,
naked to the waist, glimmer of mushroom-white flesh
in the February light of the barn; my brother, like a
referee in a boxing match, shuffles close to the action
as though he has done this for all the twelve years of his life,
born to it, born to do, to be, the man in his voice the day he curses
me for losing his blue marble, *I hope you've twins,*
*four of them, all in one go!* My body already a future
to fear, blood that's not stopped by a cold key; sorrow
and dread that I'll be a woman. The vulva pulses its signal
for my father to pull; arched back, neck, head, arms
racked, feet rooted to the ground for traction, ropes
wound through bloodless fists, the vulva
like the mouth of a child spewing; remnants
of the water sac drool like dribble, as if she's drunk,
as though she sings this new life into the world.
The vulva drawn now to its polished unwrinkled purity,
the last fierce fibres suctioning out what longs for life;
the calf's snout, eyes, ears framed in an umber aureole,
its rude, puce tongue, its tawny body a bag of bones
as it tumbles to the ground and steams; my father breathless,
hands on his hips, my brother his mirror
as they stand over all creation.

## Aama

Jodie Hollander

My Nepali aama always rose early
to make fresh chapatti for the family;
she swept the hut and fed the chickens,
and washed and dried all the morning dishes.
I watched her strong arms moving quickly,
as she changed the dirty nappy on the baby,
then went to the fields to pick soybeans.
And sometimes out there she called me
over to the well where she did laundry,
and shyly I undressed, my teenage body
little and pale in the tall monsoon grasses,
where aama filled the bucket up with water:
then she splashed and splashed and splashed me,
till I was drenched and we were laughing.
She scrubbed my body clean with rough soap,
then wrapped me up in a cotton petticoat,
and rubbed my little shoulders till I was dry,
and held me close and warm inside her arms,
which always made me cry a little bit—
But my aama did not speak a word of English,
so I couldn't tell her why I had to weep,
or explain to her about my American mother.
I kept my eyes fixed on the Himalayas,
and for a moment felt the whole world good,
and felt the earth secure, underneath my feet.

## Lagan

Niamh Prior

When he died I folded up my father
and put him in a stainless steel coffer
rowed out to sea, dropped and let him sink
a chain following fast behind, linked
it to a buoy submerged two feet below.
Looking down you could see its orange glow
as if through frosted glass, a smuggler's mooring
weighted down, padlocked, secret and secure.

I waited years until the silence was entrenched
then rowed out again, dove into cold cached
water, just a layer of skin dividing it from mine.
Sound was a solid, infused with the sigh
and whirr and click of crabs, whales and dolphins.
Against the density with bulging lungs
and chest I pulled myself down, headfirst, link
by sea-grassy link, my legs waving like

dead man's bootlaces. With a knife I scratched
off barnacles and opened the latches,
Met a pile of bones and empty spaces.
Tireless tides had washed away all traces
of flesh, left his spine bare as a bowsprit.
I stroked the crown of his skull and kissed it.
I skimmed my fingertips over his ribs,
his metacarpal bones, those coral twigs,

the palm that had held my whole torso afloat
when I was learning to kick like a toad.
– he had let his hand fall away so gently then
I didn't notice what held me was the ocean.
He had clapped and cheered as I flexed and splayed.
I'd plunged and pulled and pushed myself away,
heading straight for water out of my depth.
I closed the chest and swam up, gasping for breath.

## Dendrochronology

Alison McCrossan

Spiralling beeches lobbed to earth *were perfectly aged,*
so full in summer they laced a lucid green sky.

Ochre-golden shifts patterned the woodland floor.
The mulch of dark spells set in until spring; there

*a child astray,* with shadows of phobia in her desires,
was losing trust, and

*staggered outside,* out of words into places caterpillars go –
dandelion fields, spheres of air and seed, grass so tall

she swam with the wind into the woods to the biggest beech,
flung her arms halfway round its trunk,

looked up into fingers stretching for the light,
the thread-like veins of green heart, oxygen, promise, flow of rain,

sky to ground, root, bole, branch, leaf, sky, river, sea
waves crashed at the shore, insistent, raucous, creator of life,

eroded her pain inch by inch in painting: line, colour, stroke, daub,
word, smile,

and never did nature ask of her.
Now she sits in her car, window down, listens

to all that's gone –
echoes down faraway slopes,

transported on algae-breath to those stumps
where exposed rings map years of struggle and growth.

# Francisco and the Lobster
# Róisín Leggett Bohan

## 1st Prize, Subscriber Flash Fiction Competition

He turned the body upside down so the head lay balanced on the stainless-steel countertop. Francisco watched its tentacles twitch, its hairy legs suspended in air—opening, closing, searching for something like a seabed. He thought of grandfather in the home, the way they would tilt his armchair backwards so his feet couldn't touch the ground.

'Make sure the bands are tight.' The chef pointed to the clamped claws where the brown shell had become mottled.

They called it *controlled restraint* when he questioned the belt around grandfather's waist, it was stretched taut under his lap blanket. Francisco remembered when grandfather could walk, how he would circle the exit door of the nursing home and how once he got as far as the bus stop before they found him.

The lobster's legs stopped moving; its tail in hiding; curled under its carapace.

'Do they scream when they're boiled?' a student asked.

'No,' the chef chuckled, 'that's just gas escaping from the shell, they whip around a lot in the pot though, keep the lid on.'

Francisco looked on as the boiling water buffeted. He studied the lobster; it was still, quiet. Francisco's throat tightened, sweat escaped his armpits in rivulets. He threw off his apron and ran. He ran under the sandstone arches of Plaza Nueva, passed the noisy cafés, across the neon puddled streets, dodging trams, bicycles, taxis. He ran fast and long as the rain fell like liquid mirrors onto the shell of the lobster.

# Night Fishing

Mattie Brennan

2nd Prize, Flash Fiction Subscriber Competition

I come to this pier on the calm, clear nights, when the stars are like glitter and the moon hangs roundly. The catches are mediocre. A few mackerel when they're on the run. A pollock when I'm lucky. But the sorry truth about it is that the fishing is just to pass the time while I wait.

The boat moves along the water as a black bobbing shadow. The engine cuts and they row the rest of the way in. I leave my rod to the side and can feel the shake in my hand. From my pocket I take out a naggin of Jameson and drink a generous mouthful, let it scorch my gullet.

Their voices I'll always be afraid of. It's as if their mouths are full of gravel, and when they joke it sounds like a threat.

Any luck with the fishies?

Not a bit.

You couldn't catch a cold, hah?

They throw me the thick, wet rope, and the rough bristles scratch my palms as I tie it. They never come ashore. One feeds the bales to the other, who reaches up and gives them to me. I put this night's delivery – heroin, coke, MD, who knows? – into the back of the van. They leave as discreetly as they arrived.

I gather up my rod, my bag of bait. I set off driving towards their men in the city, cursing myself for the choices I've made in life.

# Dinosaurs

Garret Dwyer Joyce

3rd Prize, Subscriber Flash Fiction Competition

Liam had that far-away, haunted look again. He stared into the immensity of the Alberta flatlands as if someone, or something, were about to appear out of the horizon.

At first, I thought it was just the new experience of working on the prairie, that perhaps he felt like I did – a speck in the vastness of sky and land. Dust, heat and a throat-catching dryness you'd never find in Ireland.

"Is your buddy expecting the Mounties?" asked Hepburn as the afternoon freight clanked by. We leaned on our shovels, thankful for the break. "Don't worry. Drugs. Booze. In trouble with the law. Nobody gives a damn here." Years of working in the open had turned his face to shoe leather.

"Look at that," I said, pointing to the grain elevators that marked another abandoned hamlet along the track. They were battered, lifeless, but from a distance they looked like medieval towers looming out of the July haze.

"Before the water dried up, they were a sign of the good times," said Hepburn, shielding his eyes. "Won't be long now before they're all gone."

"Like the dinosaurs," whispered Liam.

Hepburn shifted his wad of chewing tobacco and spat. "You got it, pal. All that's left is bones."

A shadow passed over Liam's features.

"There's a museum in Drumheller," said Hepburn. "Entire skeletons. One of the best collections in the world."

"We'll go when we finish here," I said.

"No need," said Liam. "They're with me already."

## At the Thermopolium

Audrey Molloy

*Pompeii, 24 August 79 AD*

THEY CALL me Claudia; there are secrets I keep.
    I crush fresh coriander with a smooth estuary stone
and breathe the green scent.

Ash is in the air. It makes the drunkards cough.
    The blue amphora trembles on the shelf,
but I am not afraid.

Today I cut my palm on a sea urchin –
    you could say, deliberately –
to watch the blood fork down my arm

like the river at Ostia,
    to feel the fisherman press his mouth to a wound
that gapes like a cockle at high tide.

It is a good day to bleed. I gather
    them all morning – blue-black mussels,
oysters with petrified frills and satin innards.

Now, they simmer in the passum and harissa
    that my father hauled from Carthage.
The man standing next to me eats snails, shell and all,

the yellow juice running down his chins.
    He smells of the Lupanar. Heat rises from jars
and through the earth. The city has a taste today,

not sweat, not sulphur, but cardamom and honey
    and the sunlight sieved through plane trees
is thick and sweet. It is almost noon

and a strange cloud resembling a stone pine
    floats beyond the hills. A rain of ash and pumice begins
in this ripe moment that hangs
                                        like a pomegranate.

**Thermopolium: a street kitchen in the ancient Greco-Roman world*

## Thornley

Mark Corcoran

He was a farmer, and in toad croaks,
he demanded sunshine in one field,
and at the same bit of a moment,
up the boreen, in the next acre,
a smidgin of rain in a meadow.
Work and weather, mind and heart.
A May rainbow, icing on cloud cake,
was the champers of growth,
and the snore of a well-fed cow,
a changing of a tractor's oil.

He was like a chunky border collie,
all of the stare and obsession,
but none of the verve and hike.
And there were no words,
to call back his waddle,
when night's dew offered sap,
for the zip and light of whisky,
promised to crush him to sleep.
And there was no cake safe,
as he ate his mother's early death.

His mind, as gnarled and over barked,
as the foot of a hawthorn tree,
brought two fruits to bloom,
to the life of his mother like face.
A squint that would eat a dream
and a mouth locked to words.
Life was sweet, a honeyed thorn,
but he chewed blades of grass.

# 3rd Prize, Subscriber Poetry Competition

## Sestina for a Lost Cow

Daniel Johnson

I

Walking back from the bog,
past Sylvy's house with the yappy dog,
we saw her – a cow above the ditch
the wrong side of the slack-wire fence,
nose to nose with two dozen others, confused,
alone, cut off from the herd.

II

Remember? Walking the lane now, the herd
follows my steps, and I wonder how she crossed the bog.
In the pasture, the others were safe, if confused.
The field had turned almost red in the dog
-eared days of late August. From the fence,
heavy breath and squelching hooves ford the ditch.

III

The water gurgles in the ditch,
and the wet grass eats the sound of the herd.
I remember we waited as she fought the fence,
(the idea) staring, kicking. I imagine her lost on the bog,
doubt and terror pursuing like dogs.
She flees, dodging bogholes, confused.

IV

That summer, I was often confused,
anxious, always walking, flicking fag butts in the ditches,
flinching at tractors, yelling at the dogs,
trapped, then, in a bounded terrain. The herd,
the smell of their shit wafting over the bog.
Amazing – so many kept behind a single-wire fence.

V

How did she get through the fence?
Life proceeds against barriers, and confusion
paused us there on the sunset bog,
while all around, someone dug ditches.
(Borders.) My heart wavers, thinking of the herd.
She blocked the way up the lane. Then one dog

VI

barked (saying what?). Then the other dog
howled. And she perked up, followed the fence,
swaying massive hips, lowing deep, the herd
keeping pace, calling back, confusing
movement with freedom, breathing across ditches,
feet sunk in peat, their loving hearts deep as bogs.

VII

They move on, the cow, the herd. They bark on, the dogs.
We slowly return from the bog, and she's gone, lost along the fence.
Another year now, still confused. More water in the ditches.

# Seán Ó Faoláin International Short Story Competition

1st Prize:

€2,000

1-week residency at Anam Cara Writer's & Artist's Retreat

Publication in *Southword 44* (Spring 2023)

2nd Prize:

€500

Publication in *Southword 44* (Spring 2023)

Four runners-up will be published in *Southword 44* and receive €250 (publication fee)

The competition is open to original, unpublished and unbroadcast short stories in the English language of 3,000 words or fewer. The story can be on any subject, in any style, by a writer of any nationality, living anywhere in the world. Translated work is not in the scope of this competition.

## Deadline: 31st July 2022

Guidelines: www.munsterlit.ie

# Fool for Poetry International Chapbook Competition

1st Prize: €1,000

2nd Prize: €500

Both receive chapbook publication and 25 complimentary copies

This competition is open to new, emerging and established poets from any country. At least one of these winners will be the highest scoring manuscript entered by a debutant poet with no previously published solo collection (full-length or chapbook). Up to 25 other entrants will be publicly listed as "highly commended".

Manuscripts must be 16–24 pages in length, in the English language and the sole work of the entrant with no pastiches, translations or "versions." The poems can be in verse or prose.

There is an entrance fee of €25 for each manuscript. Entrants may enter more than one manuscript. The winners will be selected by a panel of renowned poets.

The winning chapbooks will be published by Southword Editions and launched at the Cork International Poetry Festival (2023). They will be for sale internationally through our own website, Amazon and select independent booksellers.

## Deadline: 31st August 2022

## Guidelines: www.munsterlit.ie

# Contributors

**Mara Adamitz Scrupe** is an interdisciplinary visual artist, writer, and documentary filmmaker. She is the author of six prize-winning poetry collections.

**Mattie Brennan** is a graduate of the MA in Creative Writing at the University of Limerick and has previously had work featured in *The Stinging Fly*.

**Neil Cawley** is a lawyer and writer who followed the tide from Queens to Cape Cod.

**Mark Corcoran** completed the MA in Creative Writing at Trinity. He writes poetry, stories, and is working on a novel.

**Kim Curts Mattheussens** is drawn to double rooms, doppelgängers, and dual realms. She writes from Los Angeles at bluepoet.org.

Originally from Dublin, **Garret Dwyer Joyce**'s short stories have appeared in several Canadian journals. This is his first Irish publication.

**griffin epstein** is a musician and poet working as an educator and community-engaged researcher in Toronto. Find them at: griffinepstein.com.

**Frank Farrelly** won the Rush Poetry Prize and Francis Ledwidge Award. His first collection, *The Boiler Room* (Revival Press) was published in 2020.

**James Finnegan** has a new collection of poems *The Weather-Beaten Scarecrow* due out with Doire Press in late September 2022.

**Shelley Hastings** is a writer and producer. She is the winner of The Aurora Prize for short fiction.

Born in Tipperary, based in Sligo, **Seán Hickey** writes poems and short stories. He is a freelance book reviewer for the *Irish Examiner.*

**Jodie Hollander**'s debut full-length collection, *My Dark Horses,* is published with Liverpool University Press in the UK and Oxford University Press in the US.

**Daniel Johnson** is a graduate of UCC's MA in Creative Writing. He teaches at St. Michael's College in Vermont.

**Jay Kelly**'s work is published in *The Independent* and placed amongst the winners of the Seán Ó Faoláin and Fish competitions.

**Patrick Key** lives in New York City and *The Book of Matthew* is a selection from his first novel in development.

**Peadar Lamb** is an artist working primarily in the medium of stained glass for over 20 years, employing a variety of techniques (some of which have changed little since the 11th century).

**Thomas Lawrance** lives in Ireland, where he writes fiction and performs stand-up comedy. he was recently shortlisted for the Alpine Fellowship Writing Prize.

**Wes Lee** lives in New Zealand. Her latest collection *By the Lapels* was launched in 2019 (Steele Roberts Aotearoa).

**Róisín Leggett Bohan**'s work has appeared in various places including *New Irish Writing* and Poetry Ireland's ePub '22. When she is not writing she might be seen searching for ghosts.

**Timothy McBride** published *The Manageable Cold* with TriQuarterly Press at Northwestern University. He grew up in Rochester, NY, and now lives in Cary, NC.

**Peggy McCarthy** lives in Waterford city. Her work has been published in *Fish Anthology, Hold Open the Door* and *Cork Words.*

**Alison McCrossan** is from Cork, Ireland. She writes poetry and fiction. Publications include *The Honest Ulsterman, Orbis,* and *Southword.*

**Jim McElroy:** Seamus Heaney, Francis Ledwidge, Mairtín Crawford Awards. Poetry Ireland Introductions. Award-winning chapbook, *We Are The Weather,* by Smith | Doorstop.

**John Minihan** was born in Dublin in 1946 and raised in Athy, County Kildare. His photographs have been exhibited throughout the world.

**Audrey Molloy**'s debut collection *The Important Things* (The Gallery Press, 2021) received the 2021 Anne Elder Award. She lives in Sydney.

**Kate Norris** is a writer from County Monaghan. This is her first published short story. She is currently based in Paris.

Belfast-born **Eimear O'Callaghan** won the 2018 Cúirt International New Writing Prize. She's the author of *Belfast Days* (Merrion Press, 2014).

**Jamie O'Halloran** recently won second prize in the Fool for Poetry International Chapbook Competition with *Corona Connemara & Half a Crown.*

**Ava Patel** won *Prole Magazine*'s 2021 pamphlet competition. She's been published in *Orbis* and *New Welsh Reader,* among other places.

**Niamh Prior** holds a PhD in Creative Writing. Her work has appeared in publications including *Quarryman, The Stinging Fly* and *The Penny Dreadful.*

**Gerard Smyth**'s tenth poetry collection, *The Sundays of Eternity* (Dedalus Press), was published in 2020. He is a member of Aosdana.

**Breda Spaight**'s debut poetry collection is forthcoming from Arlen House. Her chapbook *The Untimely Death of My Mother's Hens* is available from Southword Editions.

**Andrea Ward** is from Dublin. Her writing has been published in literary journals, and has won or been shortlisted in several competitions.

**Sarah Wright** lives in Yorkshire, UK and has published in the *Fish Anthology, Flash, Mslexia, Exchanges* and *Poets Meet Politics.*

**Enda Wyley**'s sixth poetry collection is *The Painter on his Bike,* 2019, Dedalus Press. She is a member of Aosdána.

# *How to Submit*

*Southword* welcomes unsolicited submissions of original work in fiction and poetry during the following open submission periods:

POETRY

| | |
|---|---|
| What to submit: | Up to four poems in a single file |
| When to submit: | 1st December, 2022 – 28th February, 2023 |
| Payment: | *Southword* will pay €40 per poem |

FICTION

| | |
|---|---|
| What to submit: | One short story (no longer than 5,000 words) |
| When to submit: | 1st January – 31st March, 2023 |
| Payment: | *Southword* will pay €250 for a short story of up to 5,000 words |

Submissions will be accepted through our Submittable portal online.
Visit www.southword.submittable.com for further guidelines.

Printed in Great Britain
by Amazon

82850921R00057